I0733527

CHRISANN DAWSON

CONGO

EBOLA

THE CONGO SERIES

BOOK 3

ISBN 978-1-953158-17-8
90000

9 781953 158178

CONGO

EBOLA

Chapter 1

James sighed.

Immediately, his mind raced back to 2011 and the life-changing experience he had that year. It was nearly all he could think about when remembering his prior encounter with Congo. While it had started with what he thought was going to be an ordinary mission, it eventually led into an unexpected reunion with the love of his life and ended with the two of them being kidnapped by rebel forces, held for ransom, and narrowly escaping with their lives. Six years ago, he had gone to finish his previous mission, and here he was on an Air France flight that was about to land him there in that very same place for the third time. While parts of his past experiences had been amazing overall, they were something he had hoped never to repeat and this assignment scared him. He knew it was because he had more to lose than the first time that he had landed in N'Jili Airport in Kinshasa. Now, he had a wife and two beautiful boys.

The sigh formed itself into a smile when he thought about Julia, and how their harrowing experience forced their relationship to blossom into something solid very quickly. Once safe, they had made their union official with a stateside wedding and short honeymoon before James was shipped back to Congo to finish that initial mission.

He was tired of adventure after that and just wanted to be with Julia. James had managed to get himself assigned to a training position for communications at Joint-Base Lewis-McCord in Washington state. Six years later, he found himself about twelve months out from being eligible for the retirement benefits that came with two full decades of service. That year should have slipped by on easy wings, until just a few days earlier when he got the phone call.

"James Worthy? This is Colonel John Fitzpatrick. Long time. How've you been?"

"Fine sir," James responded, trying to mask his quickly sucked in breath. "What's on your mind?"

"Ha! Some things never change," Fitzpatrick answered. "Always right to the point. I like that about you. I'm calling to pull you out of your life of leisure among the evergreens. We need you in Congo again but in a totally different capacity. Want to hear the details?"

"Do I have a choice?" James half teased.

"Not really," Fitzpatrick chuckled. "I'm sure you've heard the news about this most recent Ebola outbreak in Congo. Well, the international medical volunteers on the ground near the spillover spot, the interior town of Domiongo, require some oversight. They need someone in charge of security for the entire operation. Your connection to the Congo and grasp of Lingala makes you the perfect man for this job. I'll email you the details of the assignment. You can look it over and give me an answer tomorrow."

James agreed to do just that. Four days later, he was in the air and on his way. Julia was worried about him being so close to the epicenter of the outbreak of this deadly hemorrhagic fever. As a nurse, she was fully aware of the risk to her husband's health by being in such proximity. Plus, raising their boys alone nagged at her mind. James shared her concern.

Even though he considered himself to be a solid believer, the foundations of James' faith were shaken by this task. Once again, a sigh released some of his inner turmoil. He put down the information with the details of the assignment, rested his head against the seat cushion and prepared to land in Paris where he was to change planes.

Chapter 2

The jetliner was on its final descent to the airport. James could feel the wheels snap into place, preparing to touch down. He relaxed as soon as the ones in the rear contacted the runway, but immediately the plane was once again going up. Several passengers around him that were awake expressed surprise at the rapid change of plans by the pilot. All eyes turned toward the few windows that had shades open.

Several passengers shrieked in fear and exclaimed simultaneously, "We're going to die!"

James, too, saw what they saw. Another 757 was touching down on the right side of their plane, landing on a perpendicular runway. As their craft climbed upward, the oncoming plane passed just under theirs. James quickly opened his shade in time to see the other plane taxiing down the runway on the left. The two planes missed a messy collision by only inches. "Oh God, thank You," he breathed.

Several others around him also added their praise to God. One middle eastern businessman behind him was profusely thanking

Allah. Nervous energy forced all the passengers that had witnessed the event to suddenly talk to each other, recounting what they had seen. The oblivious ones awoke to learn of the near miss. Within a few minutes of circling the airport, their plane landed safely, and the passengers disembarked.

James grabbed his rucksack and followed the crowd, most stopping to thank the pilot, who himself looked a bit unnerved. Once he got to the terminal, he found a cup of coffee, a cheese sandwich, and a quiet corner in a café in the middle of the night. He wanted to wrap his mind around everything and get his thoughts focused on his current mission. Somehow, he couldn't shake the idea that the "almost accident" was a harbinger, something to hint at the risk that lay ahead of him in Congo. "What time I am afraid, I will put my trust in You," James repeated the verse from Psalm 56 to himself out loud until he felt calmer and more in control.

As a Special Forces soldier, he was always trained to keep his mind at ease and yet focused, but as he aged, he found that he needed to lean more on God's strength and less on his own.

An hour before taking off for Kinshasa, James was seated at his gate. He was exhausted from the first leg of his journey and knew that once he was in Congo, he would be immediately taken interior, where he figured that any sleep he managed would be poor. Determined to preempt that on this next seven-hour flight, he boarded the plane when his seat number was called, popped a ten-milligram chewable melatonin into his mouth, and settled back to sleep all the way to Kinshasa. He was out before they had reached cruising altitude.

Chapter 3

An hour before the plane was scheduled to land, James was awakened by the stewardess bringing breakfast and coffee. He sat up, stretched out his still well-chiseled back muscles, and worked on waking up his mind. Navigating the N'Jili Airport was never an easy task, and he had to hit the ground running.

James carefully nursed the small, very strong cup of coffee after adding his cream and sugar. He took time to check his passport, visa, and letter of intent. The last time he was in Congo, he was a part of an American unit sent by President Obama to hunt down rebel warlords. This time would be very different. He would be a small piece of a larger international community assembled to deal with this deadly crisis. It would be a new experience for him, probably requiring some mental adjustments.

Every passenger buckled in as the captain announced they were on their final descent. After the near miss in Paris, James was more than a little nervous about the prospect of landing. The worry was unfounded as the pilot smoothly set down the huge craft on the rather dilapidated field. After James secured his belt pack and shifted his rucksack onto his shoulder, he stepped out the door onto the portable metal stairs. The combined heat and humidity of the early morning in Congo engulfed him, making him feel as if he were breathing in warm bath water.

He said his final goodbye to the stewardess and civilization and walked down the steps. He was shuffled along with the others toward the terminal to be greeted by the health official checking shot records in the back of passports. Once inside, the chaos and confusion, combined with the heat, made a strange welcoming committee. James maneuvered through the crowd toward customs. He knew his international invitation would be more than enough to get him through the process easily. He stepped to the small window, handed the man his papers, and waited for them to be handed back. On the other side of the gate, he was supposed to be greeted by the United Nations' protocol.

James noticed a thin, dirty-blonde haired man with his name on a sign and walked in that direction. The man reached out a hand. "James Worthy? I'm Sebastian Smith, part of the UK delegation here in Congo to address this crisis. I'm the one who will get you on your next flight to the interior."

"Nice to meet you, though not really under these circumstances,"

James replied. "Just curious, but I studied as much as I could of Domiongo. I could not see an airport there. How exactly am I landing?"

"Good question. Well, weeks back when the international community felt the need to move in to manage this outbreak, they hired an Italian company to build a dirt runway. That's the reason only small prop planes can get in and out with ease. Larger shipments of supplies are going upriver by barge and then by road. Anything else you were wondering about?"

"What about housing?"

"Another good question," Sebastian said. "An educational facility has offered the use of their buildings as clinics, offices, and temporary dormitories. Rather primitive but better than the grass huts that many have there. No running water per se, but large plastic cisterns have been placed on elevated platforms to use gravity to create pressure for showers. Just bucket flushing for the bathrooms though. Meals and clean water are being prepared by experts. Here's your ride," Sebastian said as he led James back out onto the tarmac and up to a small prop plane.

"This is Dan Carson. He's a missionary pilot with Mission Aviation Fellowship. He's been a huge help in getting people in and out of the interior. Dan, meet James Worthy, American military, here to coordinate the security efforts out there in Domiongo."

James and Dan shook hands and exchanged information about their homes stateside. Dan took James' rucksack, placed it in the back, and said they were waiting for one more passenger. Sebastian dismissed himself and left the two men to become more acquainted.

Soon, an American-trained Congolese doctor named Pierre Kalongo showed up. Once he was situated with his gear properly stowed under the cabin, the men readied themselves for the four-hour flight to Domiongo and their uncertain future in this terrifying health crisis.

Chapter 4

Of course, the takeoff went smoothly, but James was worried about the landing on that new dirt runway. He had flown in various crafts his whole military career with little bother to his equilibrium, but he noticed, as he had aged, that his stomach did not tolerate the rough flying of smaller planes well. As Dan circled his Cessna around the field to check for goats, James felt the blood drain from his face. Things became black for a second, and he was sure he was going to be sick. He grasped the plastic bag Dan handed him and steadied his head against the seat back.

But sooner than he had expected the plane was down and the door was open, allowing a warm breeze to fan his face. James sighed his relief as he tumbled out of the plane, thankful to be safely on the ground.

Pierre was just as pleased to have landed, but the two men became gravely sober as they remembered why they were there.

One man stepped away from the small building being used as a terminal accompanied by a soldier, the strong sunlight causing them both to squint their eyes. "Hello, I'm Jim Pressman from the UK; this is Facundo Martinez, a UN soldier from Uruguay. Glad you're both here. I'm in charge of protocol in Domiongo with the international response to this outbreak. Both of you are vital to the success of this mission. James, I'm happy to turn over security to you. I've been carrying that burden in addition to my other duties. Pierre, we need your expertise on this deadly disease."

Both men put forth their hands to shake, but he put his up in protest. "New rule; no hand shaking here on the ground. We touch elbows instead. Trying whatever means necessary to prevent the spread of the virus."

James and Pierre tried out their new greeting as Dan prepared his craft to return to Kinshasa with a few outbound aid workers. Pressman led the way to an ancient Toyota Landcruiser that was parked a few meters away. "I'll drive you to your quarters, then meet you in an hour to give you a tour of the operations before the evening meal is served," he instructed. Facundo stayed behind on his post.

"This landing strip was built north and east of Domiongo only a month ago," Pressman offered as the two men threw their gear into the back of the Toyota and climbed in. James took the back seat.

"Can you explain what we're seeing as we head toward the compound?" James asked. "Was this road also repaired to accommodate the mission?"

"Yes," Pressman said. "You were here in Congo six years ago I was told. So, you are familiar with the condition of most of the interior roads. This one was in no shape to bring people and sensitive equipment along, so it was repaired by the same Italian company that built the strip. The jungle is very dense along both sides of the road, but Domiongo also has very wide-open spaces. After all, a large part of it is savannah as well."

Now it was Pierre's turn. "So, what are we to expect as far as medical conditions? What type of buildings are being used as clinics? And what protocol is there to ensure the safety of the medical staff?"

"Well, there's the Josephite school complex on the north side of town, a bit away from the main population," Pressman answered. "The year was nearly over for the dry season when the outbreak occurred, and the administrators have graciously offered the use of their compound for as long as needed. They run a technical and teaching institute here that has been in Domiongo since 1929. Some buildings are older, but all are well-maintained for the purpose of educating young people. As for the safety protocol, standard practices are being observed. Doctors and nurses are completely suited up with no skin showing. They are then sprayed down with bleach after seeing patients even before the suits are removed. So far, none of the medical personnel have been infected with the disease."

Since the school was near the airport, the drive was completed in less than ten minutes. The Toyota stopped in front of a heavy steel gate and honked demandingly. The gate swung open to allow James and Pierre to step into their new reality: combating Ebola in central Congo.

Chapter 5

The gate opened and before them sat an old, red-roofed structure. It had been built long ago as the first school of the Josephites, a small Catholic mission organization, but was eventually repurposed into school offices. Due to the current situation, however, it had been converted into a staging area and offices for the medical staff. The building was shaped like a "T" and behind it to the left was another two-story construction.

"This is where the medical community meets daily," Pressman explained. "From here they plan the day's events, record data, and execute their duties in defeating this invisible enemy. Some team members are actually doing research here on the spillover site. That building you see to the left is being used as the clinic for the infected persons. It is well away from where the rest of the volunteers, aides, and reporters are staying. We felt it best to put as much distance as possible between the volunteers and the sick."

"Good thinking," Pierre chimed in.

Once they were through the gate, and it was closed behind them, the vehicle continued down the sandy path to the left, headed toward the dorms and cafeteria. James was impressed with the quality of the buildings as they approached, and his eyes appreciated the beauty of the well-maintained grounds. Palm trees and ancient tropical plants were everywhere. Their vehicle drove past another long, two-story, red-roofed building and stopped in front of a smaller structure with a typical tin roof.

"James, this is where you and Pierre will be staying. Some security personnel are in chambers on the bottom floor over there. You have a separate room; that larger one down there on the left with the gray door. We felt like your job is rather individual and that you would do better with focusing on security if you had your own accommodations. Pierre, we have you in this first room with an American doctor, Lucas Jackson. We figured you'd enjoy a roommate that you could chat with about the States since you were educated there. He's older than you, in his forties, but you should get along."

James and Pierre hopped out, stretched their legs, and grabbed their gear. Pierre opened the door to his new home, and it was immediately obvious which bed was his by the lack of mess on the left side of the room. He had been pleased to see that it was freshly painted, had good lighting, and a wide window at the back. James, too, was pleased with his. He stepped inside to appreciate his own freshly painted pale yellow walls. It was a bit larger than the others, ten meters by ten meters, and had a double bed with a mosquito net, a wicker chair and footstool, and a long worktable and chair. There was a large open window along his back wall as well, facing a jungle twenty meters away. He set his bag down and closed the door.

Pressman had said supper would be, at five o'clock, which gave James an hour to organize himself before meeting his colleagues. Sixty minutes remained of what he considered a normal life.

Chapter 6

As James settled into his new home, he began to unpack the items he had brought with him; some out of necessity and others to give him a little familiarity to this otherwise mostly uncomfortable situation. The first thing he did was take out the picture of his family. Julia, Silas and Luke, with himself at Multnomah Falls in Oregon. It was taken only three weeks earlier, the most up to date one he had. It grieved him that his boys would be growing while he was away on this assignment. One with no definite end date. He worried that Luke would not remember him when he got back to the States, so he decided to give Julia a quick call before his life became too complicated. It was only four a.m. on the west coast, and James knew she'd be asleep, but he wanted to reassure her that he was safely on the ground.

The phone rang on the other end and Julia picked up almost immediately. "Hello?" came the groggy voice.

"Julia? Hey Babe, I just wanted you to know I'm here. Sorry to wake you."

"No worries," Julia said, clearing her throat. "I was just starting to stir anyway. How was your flight? Uneventful, I hope."

"Hmm, well, not quite. But all's well that ends well, right? We had a near miss on the stopover in Paris. Too long of a story to recount now. I'll email you about it later tonight though."

"Sounds like a plan. Just glad you're safe."

"Hey, I have my own room. It's actually a pretty good size and comes complete with its own mosquito net, too. The place, as a whole, is a large campus of a school that's almost ninety years old. You would like the architecture and landscaping. Very well maintained."

"Good," she whispered. 'But what about the important stuff? How far is the hospital facility from where you will be staying? Are you in any danger?"

James could hear the concern in her voice and was quick to put her at ease the best he could. "Don't worry, Julia. They have the living quarters as far from the medical facility as possible. A good quarter of a mile anyway. I'm fine. Besides I have no business being that close to the action."

"Well, good," Julia said, sounding the slightest bit relieved.

"Listen, I need to finish unpacking before supper in a few minutes. I promise that I will email you later when I get my laptop set up and figure out the WiFi. Take care, Babe! I love you."

"I love you too, James. Bye."

James sighed again as he clicked off the phone. His hands felt chilled, and he wiped them across his hot face. The act both calmed and comforted him. He had paid the extra money to have his American carrier open his phone to international calls and was glad he did. He finished pulling out his laptop, charging cords, and adaptors for the exchange of electrical current to 110, then splashed water on his face and brushed his hair. He was thankful his room had a sink, using gravity fed water, although no toilet or shower was in sight. He would need to find that toilet before supper.

James left his room and began to survey his environment, getting a solid lay of the complex. He had been a soldier for nineteen years, nine in the Special Forces. It was an old habit to thoroughly take in his surroundings before stepping into them. He could see Pressman chatting with a colleague across the courtyard, so he knew he had a few minutes to continue familiarizing himself with the area.

Just behind his building, beyond another long one, was a huge, sprawling breadfruit tree loaded with green, football-sized fruit, which was more like a starch, similar to a potato. Immediately to his right was a cinder block building with a rusty, tin roof. Pressman had said that it housed the media. Directly across the courtyard was a very long two-story building, and he couldn't help but wonder who was staying there. The UN, EU, and NATO all had personnel participating in this mission. There were two mango trees on either end of the building. The fruit was abundant, but it was deep green because harvest was still months away. His heart sank, hoping he was no longer in Congo to eat those ripened mangoes.

He strode across the courtyard toward Pressman and met up with him just as Pierre was stepping out of his room. Another thing that James noticed was the large step up into that longer building. From being in Congo last time, he realized that this was due to the pathways being swept daily for decades. He remembered that Congolese mamas made a habit of sweeping their yards.

James greeted the two as Pierre approached. "I hope the grand tour begins with the bathroom."

"Oh, right. I should have pointed that out when I dropped you off. Sorry, that was like an hour ago. Let's start in that direction. The bathroom is just a glorified outhouse. It's behind that building there where the press is staying. I'll walk you guys over."

"What's this long building here?" Pierre asked.

"That one actually has many uses. The cafeteria is down there on the left. It's open anytime of the day or night with water, bread, butter, jam, peanut butter, coffee and tea in thermoses, and sugar and powdered full-cream milk. To the right is an internet room, a library, and a television room. We have no channels, but plenty of DVD's and a player. The second door leads to a lounge. The rest of the rooms are used as dormitories for the international staff. Here are those bathrooms. To the right are three water closets and to the left are three showers. Those are gravity fed, but the bathrooms have buckets of water for flushing."

James stepped into one of the WC's. The ceramic floor that greeted him sloped down toward the back, leading to a hole. He did his business and washed things down by dipping a large plastic cup of water out of one of the buckets. Once outside, his small group headed back to the cafeteria for supper.

Chapter 7

Pressman, James, and Pierre entered the cafeteria, which was already mostly full. Pressman stopped to paint his colleagues a picture of the way things worked in there. "Ok, men, this is basically how it is. Most days people sit in the same few tables with the same people based on common interest or language. At those back two tables on the right are where most of the English-speaking members sit. Usually from the US or UK. They represent the International Red Cross, World Health Organization, and Samaritan's Purse. Some are doctors and pharmacists. Others are here doing data collection and research. We'll sit at that back right table."

"That sounds good to me," James piped up. "I like sitting where I can see the whole room, with my back to the wall. Even before joining the Special Forces, I liked to adhere to Doc Holliday's advice."

"You're not the first person I've heard say that," Pressman snickered before continuing. "Sitting at the two tables in that back left corner are the Congolese nurses and doctors. Pierre, you are free to join them or sit with us. I can introduce you if you like."

"Great," Pierre said. "I'll join them in a minute."

"At that middle back table are members of both the WHO and the EU. They are also here mainly organizing data and reporting results back to their offices on the continent, mostly speaking French and German. In front of them is the small contingency from the UN. They are soldiers from Uruguay, like Facundo. They all speak Spanish but are also fairly fluent in English. James, much of your job will be to work with them in security, as well as form a solid bond with the local FARDC unit. Finally, this table closest to us right here is the press corps. They represent Sky News, BBC, CNN, and Al Jazeera. They all speak several languages, including English.

"Now, on to the more important matter at hand, let me show you how food is served," Pressman continued with a grin. He began walking toward the area where the kitchen window showed a counter with plates displayed. As James followed, his right shoulder was roughly shoved back by someone passing him. A tall, bearded man with piercing blue eyes and dark brown hair gave James a long stare before mumbling an apology under his breath and moving on. James continued to watch him walk to the press table and sit down, then turned back to catch up to Pressman.

"So, the plates are filled here at the kitchen counter. The utensils are here. Dirty plates and silverware are left in this dish pan of soapy, bleach water. Drinks are here," Jim pointed toward the table to the right of the kitchen window. "Like I said, two large coolers of ice water, all purified. One of coffee. One of tea with the cream and sugar already added. Over there are the containers of additional sugar, and full cream powdered milk. Locally made fresh bread is out twenty-four hours a day, along with peanut butter, jams, and an off-brand Nutella. Grab your plates, men. James, I'll meet you back at the table. Pierre, let me get you introduced."

James made his way through the maze of cafeteria furniture and found a seat. He set his plate aside and returned for his drinks. He downed one whole cup of water and refilled it, then chose a mug of the tea as well. He craved coffee, but he also knew it was too late in the day to drink that much caffeine. Several of the English-speaking members nodded to him as he passed by again. As he settled into his chair, with his back to the wall, one man got up from the next table and sat down across from him.

"I'm Lucas Jackson, a doctor here working with Samaritan's Purse. Mind if I join you? I'd shake your hand, but especially in the cafeteria at least, we try to avoid that. Don't want to spread the virus by accident. We've gotten into the habit of bumping elbows, though."

"Yes, I heard. James Worthy, Special Forces. Just got called up to oversee the security of this operation. Nice to meet you."

"I'm glad to see a fellow American joining the team, especially doing security." Lucas began. "I tell you, there's something about this outbreak that worries me. I just can't put my finger on it."

"Well, hopefully I can," James encouraged.

"Me too," he chuckled. "So, tell me more about yourself. Like where you grew up, your military career, family...hit me." Lucas finished so his new friend could talk and began to eat his meal.

"Well," James started, "I grew up in Bucks County, Pennsylvania, just north of Philadelphia. My wife, Julia, and I went to high school together, but lost touch until six years ago when we met up in Eastern Congo. She was doing a short term as an NGO nurse at a hospital. I was here as part of that Special Forces team that President Obama sent back in 2011 to hunt down some warlords. Julia and I went through a pretty harrowing experience back then. We were actually abducted by a small rebel group."

"Wow! Sounds terrifying," Lucas responded.

"It was. We escaped though, obviously, but the experience convinced us that we wanted to be together, so we did a quick military wedding before I had to go back and finish that tour. Once completed, I got myself a cushy gig in Washington state. We have two boys, Silas and Luke, four and two."

"Yikes... at least it all worked out."

"True," James continued, "and all was going well until less than a week ago. I was called up for this assignment because I'm familiar with the culture and know a smattering of Lingala. But I gotta tell you, Lucas, I don't like it. I'm one year from retirement. I just have an uneasy feeling that something will keep me from crossing that line as smoothly as I would like. Enough about me though. Tell me your story. How long have you been with Samaritan's Purse?"

Just then Pressman approached the table after having introduced Pierre to the Congolese doctors.

"Hey," greeted Lucas. "I was just about to tell James my story." Pressman took a seat as Lucas continued. "So, I'm actually just with Samaritan's Purse for this crisis. I typically work at a hospital in Miami. Mostly, I deal with trauma in the ER, but occasionally I need to fall back on my college specialty which is infectious diseases. Sometimes people come into the port of Miami carrying more than just luggage."

"That experience makes you valuable, I'm sure," James said.

"Definitely coming in handy here. Anyway, my family lives there in Dade County. I think I'm a bit older than you, plus I married younger. I met my wife, Cindy, at our church's singles' ministry about ten years ago. We have two kids too, but a son and a daughter. Congo is new to me. Samaritan's Ministry reached out from a tip from a friend, who overheard something in a conversation. You know how that goes," Lucas smiled wryly.

"That's how I got here too," James added.

"Anyway, I'll chat more about my worries after a bit. Let's eat."

The three men dug into their plates of a very typical meal: beans, rice, greens, stewed goat, and canned corn. Pressman explained that the food repeated itself on a similar pattern each day and week. James simply appreciated a warm meal, and as the food settled into his stomach, a deep, overpowering fatigue enveloped him. His flight had begun yesterday morning in Washington. Now at the end of his second day, he was near exhaustion. He completed his meal, said goodbye to his dinner companions, and excused himself for the night. He knew that he had to get that promised email in for Julia before succumbing to his weariness.

"Well, that's a wrap for me, fellas. I'm bushed. I'll probably be up in the middle of the night thinking about what I can snack on and being irritated by the time change. See you in the morning."

James made sure he got in one more trip to the WC before retiring to his home away from home to finish off his evening.

Chapter 8

James felt immense relief when he walked into his room and locked the door behind him. He was exhausted, not only from his traveling, but also from the burden of meeting new people and adjusting to the new surroundings. His years in Washington state had softened him. He acknowledged that he was no longer as sharp as he was during his active years in the Special Forces. He also had to face his underlying fear concerning this assignment, but that would have to wait until after a night of rest.

The first thing he did was shed his shoes for the flipflops that he pulled out of his rucksack. He then got everything ready inside his bed and arranged the mosquito net, getting it properly tucked in. Next went his water bottle from the airplane, a flashlight, his Bible, pens, and his journal, a habit which he learned to appreciate from his wife. He was missing her and couldn't wait for the next time he was able to communicate with her. Thinking of Julia made him smile. His love for her was deep and had almost already lasted a lifetime. This, of course, prompted him to move onto his next task of getting connected to the internet.

One of the news agencies, realizing how vital internet was to their journalists, had worked hard to set up an independent connection through satellite phones and a series of routers that linked to the cell tower located a few kilometers away in Domiongo. Congo had jumped from the old, black rotary phones to cellular technology overnight. What used to be only ham radios and a few Motorolas, was now a sophisticated network of towers crisscrossing the country, many built by CCT, a Chinese communication company. James was really appreciating that advancement at that moment.

He sat in front of his laptop and pulled out the piece of paper from his shirt pocket that Pressman had given him with instructions on how to link to the internet. Within a minute he was excited to be connected and immediately began his letter to Julia.

```
    Hey Babe!


    I got connected pretty quick. I just
    got back from supper and decided to
    lock myself in early for the night.
    So far, I like the team members
    that I've become acquainted with.
    A man named Jim Pressman met us at
    the small, dirt landing strip, got
    us settled in, and then took us to
    the cafeteria. I ate with him and an
    American named Lucas Jackson who's a
```

doctor with Samaritan's Purse. I think I'm really going to like him.

I promised I'd tell you about that scare we had in Paris. In short, our pilot had touched down our back wheels, but suddenly changed his mind and took us straight up again, hard. A few of us who were awake looked out the window to the right and saw a jet landing on an adjacent runway. It missed ramming the side of our plane by inches and seconds. Really scary. Oddly, it seemed like a warning. You know I'm not superstitious, but I was annoyed by that thought.

Anyway, supper was nice, and I like that I have my own room. I probably will save my shower for the morning. I'm craving sleep right now. It's been a long thirty hours. Jules, please pray for me often. I'm really worried about this assignment. Give the boys a squeeze for me.

I love you, Babe.

Me

James sighed when he pushed the send button, that irritating habit that started six years ago and seemed to be a part of his Congo experience. He had one more email to send before he could begin to relax. Colonel Fitzpatrick had asked him to let him know that he was safely on the ground. He plunked out a quick correspondence to him and clicked his computer shut. . He sighed again, looked around his room, and thought about those granola bars in the bottom of his sack.

He pulled one out, replaced his clothes with gym shorts, put his shirt and pants on the hooks, and crawled into the mosquito net. He had already positioned the fan inside, tucking the net everywhere else around the bed.

His intention was to journal first, but as soon as his head hit the pillow, he felt the need for sleep rise up. As he was drifting off, he thought he heard a helicopter landing somewhere nearby. *That's a strange sound this late in the day*, was his last thought before finally giving in to slumber.

A ten-minute drive away, on that same grass landing strip, the helicopter pilot was helping his passenger, a willowy, thirty-something woman, down to the ground. She grabbed his hand to steady herself and let a few choice swear words describe what she thought of the intense heat and humidity. A thin, rigid, tall man walked over from the small mudbrick building to greet her. The Congolese soldier he had paid to keep his mouth shut, glanced away to avoid becoming even more complicit than he already was.

"I'm JP Walker," she introduced herself. The man accepted her information but offered none of his own. He simply pointed to an old Toyota pickup truck and helped JP into the passenger seat, tossing her bags in the bed.

Once they pulled out of the landing strip compound and headed for town, the driver spoke. "Are you sure you know your assignment?

We can't afford any mistakes. This man must be distracted from doing his job."

"I understand. This isn't my first rodeo," JP practically shrieked.

The rest of the ride to the older, Belgian-built houses on the north side of Domiongo was finished in silence. When they arrived at their destination, JP was introduced to the sentinel and cuisinier before being shown to her room. Without a goodnight, the two parted, each completely focused on their task. J.P. went to sleep, but her driver hung around in the shadows and then, a few hours later, slipped away from the house.

As James was falling asleep in Congo, Julia was back home and pulling out her family journal. This particular one was where she shared her fears and triumphs and all the beautiful little things that made up her life. She took her pen and added to it.

```
June 5, 2017

God, I'm addressing this as a prayer
to You because I am so frightened.
The last time I felt this way was
when James and I were abducted, but
I haven't been so terrified since.
James is far away from us and in a
very dangerous situation. Ebola,
God! Ebola! How can he combat an
unseen enemy?

Lord, I know I have to trust him to
Your care. I am completely powerless
here to do anything to help him
where he is. Lord, You must surround
```

Him with Your protection. Not only
with Yourself as a shield from that
awful virus, but also if You could
surround him with people who will love
him, and respect him, and selflessly
aid him in this task of security.

God, I love this man that You gave me.
He is a tender husband and beautiful
father to our boys. Bring him home to
us. Please don't let us be without
him in this life. God, I beg You.

Julia's plea ended with a tear that smudged her page. She
brushed it away with a bit of frustration at seeing the paper marred.
She closed the journal, closed her eyes, and internally continued her
prayer for James.

Chapter 9

James was suddenly awake, even though he had taken melatonin, knowing that it helped to readjust his circadian rhythm after traveling through several time zones. He didn't move and barely breathed. Something had startled him. Without moving a muscle, he slowly let his eyes scan the darkness of his room. Nothing seemed out of the ordinary. He then checked the open screened window on the right, but all seemed well. The distant, dim light from the cafeteria showed nothing was there. Then, slightly changing the position of his head, he looked at the screened window behind him. Although it was dark on that side of the building, bouncing flashlights in the distance showed the silhouette of a person standing just outside his room.

He was undecided on whether he should confront the peeping tom or ignore him. He chose the latter, even though he could not figure out why someone would be looking in his window. Without facing that direction, James sat up and turned on his flashlight. The quickly retreating footsteps and a snapping twig finished the story.

James glanced at his watch. Almost four a.m. He knew that going to bed early would result in him waking up early as well, but he did not expect a middle-of-the-night curiosity seeker to be involved. Regardless, he was up and decided to start his day.

Before hopping out of bed, James took the time to check the floor around his flipflops for creatures. As tough as he was, a large spider was his kryptonite. Fortunately, all was clear. He got up and pulled both window curtains shut before clicking on the overhead light. An illuminated room, where every corner could be easily seen, was an immediate comfort. James took a minute to finish unpacking his clothes. A large wooden cabinet seemed the only place to store things. He hung shirts, pants, and shorts, and placed undergarments and toiletries on the shelves to the right. He was not required to wear his standard uniform, but rather was sent with camouflage, tan, and brown shirts, and matching pants. The U.S. did not want him to be expressing obvious patriotism since it was an international response.

Finally, James drank most of his bottle of water and put his shower things in a tote that the compound had provided with the room. He gingerly opened his door and looked around. Everything was dark except the cafeteria. Even from this distance he could see a few early risers sipping on drinks. He shined his flashlight into the darkness in front of him, closed his door, and began the trek to the showers. He rounded the corner of the press dormitories, went to the bathroom first, then walked up to the first shower door.

Once inside with the door locked, James strategically placed his flashlight and proceeded to take the coldest shower he had experienced in many years. "I *am* getting soft," he told himself, as he shuddered and spit out the frigid water from his mouth. Having gotten past the initial shock, he suddenly realized how alive he felt. With his hair and body now clean, he dried off, dressed, and headed back to his room.

James finished organizing his things, made the bed, and grabbed his Bible, journal, pen, and flashlight. Determined to acquaint himself with early mornings in the cafeteria, he crossed the courtyard in seconds and entered the brightly lit room.

Chapter 10

Immediately upon entering the building, James locked eyes with the man who had bumped shoulders with him the evening before. He decided to introduce himself.

"Good morning. I'd shake your hand, but I guess that's discouraged here. I'm James Worthy. I'll be overseeing security for this operation."

"Victor Archer," the man said, standing up. "I remember you from last night. Sorry I bumped into you. I was in a hurry. I work with Sky News. Here reporting on the outbreak."

The apology surprised James. "No worries. Listen, I'm going to take some time to nurse a cup of coffee while I wake up and do some journaling. Afterward, could I sit with you for a bit?"

Victor nodded his assent, and James went to get some coffee and fresh bread which was still warm to the touch. His mouth watered as he watched the melting Irish butter, made from milk derived from grass-fed cows, making its fat content higher and the consistency extra creamy. A second piece he spread with the local peanut butter. He knew that peanuts were a staple in Congo. They were roasted and ground into a butter but lacked the salt and ingredients to make it creamy. He took his breakfast appetizer and headed to the corner table where he had sat the previous evening. After a good night of sleep, albeit a bit shorter than he would have liked, an invigorating shower, and hot food in hand, he was feeling more awake before he even sat down.

James opened his Bible to his favorite warrior battle in 1 Samuel 17 and read the story of David and Goliath. He thoroughly loved David's enthusiasm for a good fight and a just cause. James completely understood, having himself always shared the same feeling. He almost leaped at the opportunity, just as David had run toward Goliath. He finished with writing Psalm 18:2 at the top of his journal page, right under the date. Warrior King David often recorded his battle sentiments in the Psalms. In this verse, David completely elevated God as his defense, even calling Him his "High Tower." With God's help, David could see over his enemies and was best suited to assess their weaknesses.

James savored each sip of coffee and bite of bread before finishing up and heading back to Victor's table.

"Is this a good time?" James asked. "I don't want to interrupt anything."

"No, no, sit down," Victor welcomed. "I finished sending a report last night. I'm just checking my social-media accounts. I'm a confessed Twitter-aholic."

"Twitter-aholic? I didn't even know that was a thing. Although, I do like Twitter. Instagram too." James felt a little more at ease as he slid into the hard, plastic chair. "So, where are you from?"

"Well, I'm based out of London," Victor replied. "I have a flat there, not too far from the Sky News offices, but I grew up in a smaller community in the northern part of England. My family still lives there. We've had the estate for generations." He paused, and a strange look passed over his eyes. "My family is a bit of an enigma...even to me."

"Well, every family has some quirks," James said.

"This goes way beyond a few eccentricities," Victor dismissed before trying to move on. "How about you and your family? I found your Twitter profile. Bio says you grew up in Pennsylvania but live in Washington State and that you're a Christian with almost twenty years of military experience. I'm curious how you were able to consistently maintain your faith in such a difficult career field."

"Umm, not sure how to answer that," James said. "I've been a Christian since I was about eight, and I was rather open about my faith in high school, but during my early military years, I really just kept my mouth shut and did my job. I wasn't preachy, but I wasn't hiding my faith, either. I was there if a friend needed to talk, and they all knew that; respected that. But as I've gotten older, and especially since I've been married, I've grown very serious about everything."

"Why did marriage change that?" Victor asked.

"My wife Julia is the best. Her own unwavering, out-and-out faith has really influenced me to be more vocal about sharing Christ." James paused and Victor jumped in.

"How long have you been married?"

"Six years. Julia and I went to high school together, then didn't see each other for quite some time before we were reunited in eastern Congo, of all places. I was part of that mission when President Obama sent Special Forces soldiers down here to hunt a notorious warlord. Julia was doing a short-term medical mission as an NGO nurse. We were actually abducted by a rebel militia and held hostage for a week. That really elevated our relationship to the 'serious' stage a lot more quickly than it probably would've gotten there otherwise."

"Oh, my goodness. I overheard Pressman explaining that to someone last night after you had gone to your room but didn't catch all the details. I'd like to hear that story sometime. So, it sounds like you were a bit older when you got married. Like what? Thirty or so?"

"Yeah, thirty-one, actually," James said. "Julia is the same age as me. There were some adjustments after both living on our own for so long, but it was totally worth it. What about you? Married?"

"Nope. And I'm really old," Victor confessed. "A year older than you or more. Just turned thirty-nine last month. Honestly, I guess I've hesitated to get married because of my family. My kind of girl does not fit their picture for me."

"How so?" James asked.

"I come from old money, and all the complications that entails, but what I really want is simplicity. My family expects me to marry specifically to carry on the tradition of passing that money on to the next generation. I want to find someone who just wants to be with me for me, not for the money. No agenda."

"How could anyone object to that?"

"You don't know my family," Victor cautioned. "My parents are in control of absolutely everything. Right down to choosing who I marry."

"Sounds invasive," James admitted.

"Very. I'm sorry, I didn't mean to unload on you like that. Especially since we just met."

"No, no, it's cool. We all have stuff we have to deal with. That's what makes us human."

By the time their conversation was winding down, the sun had begun to rise and, slowly, other team members were starting to trickle in. James kept his eye on the room and its inhabitants, but he had to admit that his curiosity about Victor's family was piqued. When he saw Lucas come in, he excused himself, grabbed a plate, piled on a true breakfast meal, and joined his new friend at what was becoming their typical table in the back corner.

Chapter 11

James enjoyed finishing his breakfast with Lucas. It was only the two of them until they noticed Pressman approaching the table. Before he got there, James whispered, "Sometime I want to hear more on your fears about this mission. Maybe we can sit down together after supper for a while."

"Sure. Tonight works. I can try to find a corner in the lounge so we won't be interrupted."

"James, if you're finished," Pressman began as he walked up to them, "I may hand you off to Facundo and our local point man, Katey. He's the head of our Domiongo region Congolese unit. I arranged for them to take you on a tour of the perimeter of the compound. Seemed like a good place to start. Hope you've got some good walking shoes. I thought we'd begin with that. I'm guessing you'll be finished about ten, so I'll meet you back here around then to discuss your job description and goals."

James stood and stretched out his back muscles. He started to extend a hand to say good-bye to Lucas, nearly forgetting the new protocol, but quickly stuck out his elbow to correct his mistake. "Talk to you later," he stated as he followed Pressman across the room and out the front door of the cafeteria.

In the courtyard, Facundo stood chatting with Katey. Pressman introduced James, who again had to remember not to shake hands.

"Nice to meet you, Katey," James began, waving his hands as a substitute greeting. "Oyebi Lingala? Ngai, nayebi mwa ndambo."

The head of the Congolese unit was excited to hear that James knew Lingala. He grinned broadly and then responded, "Eeh, nayebi Lingala malamu, kasi nayebi Anglais mpe. I do also speak English, but since Facundo does not know Lingala, and neither of us know Spanish, I believe we must use a language everyone can understand to avoid any miscommunication. Besides, I never get to practice American English, so this is good!"

Facundo piped up. "I only know little English so please, very slowly."

"Absolutely," replied James. "No problem. What's the plan?"

"My goal is to start at the front gate and walk the whole property clockwise. James, do you need to change shoes first?"

"I do, actually. I'll be back in two minutes."

James quickly returned with hiking boots, a pad and pen, and the simple smell of the light coconut from his sunscreen. "Ready now.

Let's go."

The men began by walking back to the front gate, which only took a few minutes.

"So, is there anything about the security of this operation that worries either of you?" James asked.

Katey piped up as they took the narrow path northward that followed the inside of the wall. "Yes! I am very worried. Not as much about the physical security, although I do want to point out some weaknesses, but I am truly afraid about the tension in the village of Domiongo about this outbreak. Many are terrified. Those who have loved ones who are sick here at the clinic are saying that proper protocol is not being followed. They are speaking of this in all the markets in the village. Others who have already had family die are saying that they are not being permitted to bury their dead according to tradition."

"Hmm. I wonder why they feel that standard safety procedures are not being followed. Does it have to do with clinical or medical safety, or are they speaking of something else?"

Suddenly the pathway narrowed, forcing the men to walk single file, and Katey paused before responding to show James something. "Do you see this large mango tree? It has long branches that cross over the wall to the road on the other side. It would be very easy for someone to climb over into the compound by crawling on that tree.

This is one thing that must be fixed. People will need to be hired to trim back all trees from near the perimeter walls."

James agreed to Katey's suggestion and made a note in his tablet.

"Now, to answer your question, the broken protocol I am speaking of is medical. This may be a rumor, but it is whispered that they do not wash between patients. It is not only the washing of the medical staff after they are finished seeing patients though, it is also that they are not taking safety precautions within the clinic walls."

"There any proof about a disregard for safety? What exactly is standard practice for going from one patient to another?"

Katey answered the question with a suggestion, "I think that Dr. Jackson will be more knowledgeable. My sources are only the gossipers in the city."

Facundo, interrupting, pointed to something high up in a bonyanga tree. "See. Way up there near the top. A small clan of monkeys. What exactly are those, Katey?"

"They are called 'lesula' by some. The species is new to western man. I believe that although many hunters in Congo have known this monkey forever, it was only discovered back in 2011 or 2012. I cannot remember the exact date. I have never seen one in this area of Congo. Actually, I have never seen one. My grandfather was a skilled hunter. He told me of this as a young child."

The density of the forest rapidly increased as they continued.

Although it was the beginning of dry season, the monsoons had only stopped a week earlier. The heavy smell of the damp, pungent earth attacked James' nose. The fragrance immediately took him back to his and Julia's abduction. On that first night, when they had been force-marched to the rebel camp, a recent storm had acquainted him with the aroma of damp jungle. He was always surprised by the strength of smell to bring back a memory.

Trying to move past the unpleasant thoughts, James chimed in. "Isn't it unusual for monkeys to be so close to the human population?"

"Very good point, sir," Katey said. "I am surprised to see them here, as if they are comfortable around man. What you say is valid."

They were way past the compound buildings and began to head east, almost directly behind the cafeteria. The path widened and suddenly the wall was gone, leaving only a chain-link fence, just as the forest gave way to a clearing, roughly three hundred meters wide, before the forest once again engulfed them.

"Where did the wall go? Is this only fencing, Katey?" James asked. "Is anyone worried about this?"

"Yes," both men answered at once. Katey picked up, "The property did not originally have a wall completely around it. When the epidemic broke out, the response team hastily put up this temporary fence."

Facundo added, "I do not believe it is sufficient to keep out anyone who would attempt to enter. I believe that it should have a razor wire on top."

Both James and Katey agreed with that. James added that in his notebook.

Soon the path turned south. Once again, the jungle was dense and smelled strongly of damp foliage. Just before the final turn took them west back toward the main gate, Katey pointed out a vine-covered entrance, remarking that the path on the other side was a back way to the village and that the gate had not been used for years.

James bumped elbows with the men to conclude their task and made an appointment to meet with them again an hour before supper. He headed back to his room to rest before his meeting with Pressman. It was only nine a.m., and he was already drenched in sweat, but his first official task as head of security was complete.

Chapter 12

James had one hour before his appointed meeting with Pressman, and he had several thoughts nagging him. First, he could not get over the fact that someone had been peeking in his window and he was determined to find out who it was. Second, he was struggling to identify the sound he heard just before dozing off. And now, he was wondering about that clan of monkeys.

Shaking his head to try and focus, he grabbed his water bottle that he had filled up earlier and plopped himself on the wicker chair in his room with his phone, journal, a larger notebook, and several pens. He was just getting comfortable to prepare for a good thinking session when it occurred to him to check the area outside his window. He pulled himself out of the chair and walked around the back of his room.

There was very little foliage near his window, just a few random weeds. And although the sandy soil was relatively dry from lack of precipitation, he could clearly see two footprints close to the window that were deeper than the ones moving away from it. He bent down to ascertain any distinguishing marks, but all that was obvious were three circles in the same pattern as commonly seen on the bottom of most flipflops.

"Huh. Nothing unique about that in the Congo," James said out loud. He took another minute to follow the retreating prints toward the jungle that framed the building on that side. Almost up to the point where the path started into the forest, James noticed that a deeper bootprint was visible. It appeared as if the flipflop wearer stopped to connect with a soldier, police officer, or armed guard. Those were the only personnel James knew who would frequently wear heavy boots in the Congo. This nagged at his mind as well, as he returned to his room and chair to resume his meditating.

He first opened his big notepad. It had blank pages on one side and lined on the other. He took a pencil and ruler, drew out the perimeter of the compound as close to scale as he could get it, and filled in the buildings as he had seen them. He noted where the trees needed to be trimmed back and the place in the forest where they had spotted the lesula monkeys. He then marked an X at the window behind his room and an arrow pointing in the direction of the retreating footprints. He thought again about the path near the wall on that side of the compound and knew that there was a locked entrance that opened to another one that led to the northwest part of

Domiongo village.

He decided to put a pin in that and transitioned his thoughts back to the monkeys. He couldn't figure out why they were inside the walls of the compound, and why they seemed so comfortable being that close to humans. Wanting to learn more, he moved from the chair to the long worktable and opened his laptop. He needed to do some research on this species and their unique qualities. Unfortunately, the ones he glimpsed today were too distant for a good inspection.

Wikipedia was always the easiest link to find, and James opened an article on the lesula monkey. He began perusing its contents, learning first that it was considered an "old world monkey." He made a note to himself to look up that term.

"Well, Katey was nearly correct," James said out loud to himself, a habit he'd formed when learning a new subject. It continued as he began to read the article aloud. "The lesula was made sensationally known to the world in 2012, but it was first discovered by westerners in 2007 in the town of Opala, where one had been tied to a post as a pet. It wasn't until 2012 that the media's attention was caught." *Hmm,* James thought, silencing himself. *I wonder why it took westerners so long to see this monkey. Traders and missionaries have been in this country for centuries. Very odd.* He turned off his inner dialogue and returned to reading the article. "The males have a blue back side, and the species has very human-like qualities to the look of its face."

James stopped for a minute. He was chewing on why this small troop of monkeys, and a rare species at that, was so close to the epicenter of the Ebola outbreak. A disturbing thought entered his mind that he attempted to push away without success. *What if these monkeys had been used for experiments or research? What if one of them was infected? What kind of destruction could spread as a result?* He wiped his hand across his forehead as if it would remove the thought. A quick glance at his watch showed that it was almost time to meet Pressman for an overall job description and objective. He made a note to ask Katey about a two-way radio operator in the village or a way to buy a cheap disposable phone. He wanted information.

Chapter 13

James opened the door to his room, peered out, then closed and locked it behind him. This was the first time that he decided that locking was a good idea. He had this strange feeling that something was not right. The combined recent events were sending up whispered warnings and sounding mental alarm bells. He felt his muscles tense up and his gut do a somersault.

Walking over to the cafeteria to fill his water bottle and get both a small cup of coffee and a slice of bread with peanut butter, James knew he only had ten minutes before his meeting with Pressman. As he stepped into the large room, he noticed that all the tables had been cleaned up from breakfast. A few, like him, were looking for some mid-morning calories and hydration. He didn't see any of the Americans, though. As he passed the kitchen window, he heard someone call his name. James turned to see a familiar Congolese face, albeit more mature than the last time they had seen one another. "Kongolo? Is that you? I can't believe it! What are you doing here?"

"I am working here," Kongolo replied, almost too shocked to speak. Recovering, he continued, "Since I last saw you, I have married and moved to the village of Domiongo. I wanted to be far from Eastern Congo and the unrest. My wife and I have two small boys. I had to earn income somewhere, so when I heard from my cousin of this job, I applied and got it."

"Working in the kitchen?" James asked, a little surprised that Kongolo was okay with such domestic employment.

"Well, I mean, it wasn't my first choice, but with a family to provide for, I had to take what I could get. It is woman's work, but I am not ashamed. The money is very good."

"I get it," James replied. "I have two boys as well. Fathers have responsibilities, so good for you."

"Thank you, James. Now, what about you? I thought once you left Congo you would not return."

"Same here. I had no intention of coming back, but I was called out of a teaching job to come do security for this international response. I'm actually very glad that you're here. I believe that before this assignment is finished I'll need some trusted Congolese friends. I'll talk to you again later. I have a meeting to get to."

He took a minute to fill a plastic plate with bread; some with peanut butter and jam, others with peanut butter and hazelnut spread. He downed some water, filled his bottle, and fixed a coffee. He balanced everything on his notebook and headed two doors down to the lounge.

It was his first time completely inside the room. He took a moment to study the lay of it, the furniture, and the position of the windows and doors. Pressman had not yet arrived. James chose a simple couch with a coffee table in front and put down his refreshments. He organized his notebook, pens, and pencils. Just then, Pressman walked in. James stood up to shake hands but finally remembered at the last second just to wave in greeting.

"Howdy."

"Hey, James. How was your hike around the perimeter? Anything noteworthy?"

"Sure. A few things. Do you mind if I go through the notes I took?"

"Go ahead," Pressman offered in his softly spoken British accent, "and seriously, if something bothers you, please let me know. It's your job to take care of security, but I am also answering to colleagues higher up the food chain, so to speak."

"Of course. Well, first is the need to cut back some overhanging trees. In several locations along the western wall, following the road, they are hanging over it which gives easy access to any good climber who wants into the compound. Katey noticed it and pointed it out to me. How do I go about hiring someone for the task of cutting back the branches?"

"I believe you can work directly with Katey and the local FARDC army on that. What else?"

"There is a new part of the perimeter that is only chain-link fence. It is not very tall or secure. We all felt that razor wire needed to be added to the top."

"I would be surprised if that could be purchased nearby," Pressman noted. "But maybe the compound has some lying around. There's an ancient depot behind this building. Give that a look. Otherwise, maybe you could email Sebastian and see if he has a contact in the capital that could expedite a shipment."

"One more thing. As I was drifting off to sleep, I thought I heard the distinct sound of a helicopter. Did one land here last night?"

"A helicopter?" Pressman snickered, a little too condescending for James' taste. "That is highly unlikely. No one outside of the response community has access to the field. I'm sure it was just a part of your dreams, James. Nothing to worry about." Pressman finished and took a quick glance at the floor.

Suddenly James was wary. The action of looking down while speaking often meant that a person was being dishonest. *Is Pressman hiding something?* he wondered.

"So," James restarted, "aside from what I've discussed, what are your overall objectives for me?"

"Here's a typed-out report form and another sheet with general duties," Pressman responded. "Mainly, I need you to get to know everyone; their routines, why they're here, and which organization they represent. Be aware of the general schedule of the operation."

"Okay."

"Then pay attention to the physical security duties like your local and UN personnel; their shifts, locations, and so forth. I also want you to know this compound like the back of your hand. Memorize each path."

"Good," James said.

"Every week, I want this form filled out and emailed to me. It's not necessary for you to report to your own military superiors, but you are permitted if you feel like you need some advice. That about sums it up," Pressman said standing. "I have a meeting with the press corps in five minutes. I'm glad we were able to get this started right away this morning so we can get after some of these things. Looks like we're headed in the right direction. How are your accommodations? Everything all right?"

"Yes, of course." James said as he rose to say goodbye. He sat back down on the couch to think about their conversation as he finished his bread and drink. He made mental notes of the details, primarily Pressman's strange behavior when he had mentioned the helicopter. James couldn't help but wonder if it was real or if, perhaps, he was just being paranoid. He had hoped his meeting with Pressman was going to provide answers, but it seemed like it was causing more questions instead.

Chapter 14

Pressman left his meeting with James more than a little disturbed. He felt like he was being pressured from two sides, two factions hoping for two very different outcomes of the response to this Ebola outbreak. Just as he was reaching his door, he received a phone call from a number that he did not recognize, but the international exchange indicated that it originated somewhere in the United States. Apprehensively, he answered. "Hello? Who's this?"

"Are you going to have trouble keeping up your end of the bargain?" the voice on the other end asked icily.

"What do you mean? Who is this?" Pressman answered.

"Let's just say that this is a concerned third party. You've been placed there in Domiongo for a specific purpose. Don't go getting distracted by that security officer the U.S. put there. He is nothing. His concerns carry no weight in the overall scheme of things. Do you understand? Part of your job now will be to keep him from doing his job well."

"Who is this?" Pressman barked. "Identify yourself."

"My name is of no concern. It's our agenda that you should be worried about. You already know all we need you to for the moment. Expect a new team member to show up in the next couple of days, no questions asked or answered. Am I clear?"

"Of course." Pressman's voice sounded strained as he realized it was best if he just conceded. The connection clicked off, leaving him staring at his phone. He pursed his lips, and his furrowed brow expressed his frustration.

"How did I get myself into this mess?" he nearly shouted.

With that he sat down and wrote out a long, hand-written letter to his wife back in the U.K. He assured her of his love and said he hoped to see her again soon. Feeling overwhelmed by thoughts of fear and self-doubt, he got up and put the letter on his bedside table. He decided he'd read it over one more time before sending it and then slumped down into his chair. It was going to be a long day.

❧

James put his feet up on the coffee table, grabbed his plate and cup, and leaned back on the sofa. He decided that it was time for an internal interrogation.

Examiner: *James, are you sure that Pressman is lying about the helicopter?*

James: *Well, he did rephrase the question before he answered. Plus, he refused to make eye contact when he brushed off the idea of a helicopter landing without the mission knowing anything about it. That, to me, seems as if he's hiding something.*

Examiner: *Yeah, but what?*

James stopped the conversation he was simulating in his mind, uncertain of how to proceed. He took his dishes to the kitchen to plop into the soapy bleach water and headed back to his room. It was only a bit after eleven o'clock. Lunch wasn't until twelve. He wanted to think on paper without being interrupted or questioned.

For some reason, he could not get those monkeys out of his mind. Something still felt off about their presence in the compound. He wondered who he should bring in on that agenda item. He had questions, but he was not sure who he could trust with even hints of his suspicions. He thought about Kongolo. He also thought about Katey. He felt as if Kongolo could be trusted more because of how much he owed James for his freedom. And even though he had only met Katey that morning, his gut told him that he could be brought into a position of confidence. But he decided to simply learn his job for a week or two, get to know Katey better, reestablish his relationship with Kongolo, and then decide how to proceed. Even though he originally wanted to journal or plot out his stream of consciousness, he suddenly found himself afraid of someone getting their hands on his writings, so he decided to keep everything catalogued in his mind for the time being.

His hour alone sped by on the flow of his thoughts. It was ten minutes until lunch started. James walked over to the cafeteria, said hello to Kongolo, and downed two glasses of water before refilling his cup with the sweet, creamy tea; so sweet that it was like having dessert before the main meal. Lunch was a nearly all-bean chili, plus corn bread served with butter. Syrup pitchers were on every table creating the opportunity to turn the corn bread into a sweet treat. The meal must've been a surprise because he witnessed people around the room exclaiming over the flavor and uniqueness of it.

James once again sat with Lucas and the other American team members. They kept their chatter light over lunch. When he was finished, he confirmed his post-supper chat with Lucas and headed to the WC before returning to his room. He recognized that a strong desire for an afternoon rest was a part of living in a tropical climate, and he decided to succumb to the call. His body was still weary from his travels, from the switch in time zones, and from his early start. He laid on the bed, turned the fan on full blast, and set his alarm to go off in an hour. Quicker than he could have imagined, James was out.

Chapter 15

James heard a strange beeping sound, as if from a distance. It took a full thirty seconds before he could remember where he was. He considered reaching over and hitting the snooze button on his phone alarm, afraid that if he turned it totally off, he would konk back out and oversleep. But instead, he just rolled over and got out of bed. Stretching, he stood for a minute in front of the fan without his shirt on to cool off. A tropical nap often finished with the person waking in a pool of sweat. He stood there until the temperature difference raised goosebumps on his chest.

Acknowledging he needed a new shirt, he hung the old one on the back of his chair to dry out and pulled a simple tan tee out of the wardrobe. Once dressed, he combed his hair, took a look in the mirror, and headed out the door to explore the depot. He knew it was behind the kitchen end of the long building, and he was hoping to catch another word with Kongolo.

As he rounded the structure on the western side, he came to an open door behind the kitchen, peeked his head inside, and asked for Kongolo. When told that he was home in the village for a break, James walked another thirty feet to an ancient mudbrick building with a rusting tin roof. The door was not bolted, and James found that it opened easily on freshly oiled hinges. He wondered about the upkeep of the grounds and who could have had oiled the door.

As hot as the tropical afternoon was outside, inside was immensely more oppressive. No air moved. The stifling heat and dank smell from old supplies almost nauseated him. Realizing that he was becoming soft, he decided he needed to soldier up.

With the door propped open behind him by an old truck battery, James did a cursory assessment of the inside of the depot. Organized and neat would not be good words to describe it. The depot appeared to be a jumbled mess of various maintenance supplies and lawn and gardening equipment. He looked for a light switch, or even simply a lone light bulb hanging from an electrical cord with a pull chain, but found neither. A single window on the other side of the room would be the only light source besides the open door. He followed the thin, windy path through the junk to the other window and forced open the wooden panel that covered it. Immediately, light and fresh air flooded the room and, thankfully, a bit of a breeze.

James knew his main job at that moment was to locate razor wire, but he decided he might as well list out all the things he saw that might prove useful in managing security. He pulled out his notebook and pencil, made a heading at the top that read, IMPORTANT, and began listing things that could come in handy. He noted how many shovels, axes, and hatchets were in the room. He listed old cans of turpentine, hard-as-a-rock bags of cement, an old hand crank drill and drill bits, hammers, screwdrivers, and crow bars. He saw nothing directly related to security, but he knew that any of these items could be helpful in an unplanned emergency.

James also made a secondary list of unusual things he came across like an old road sign that looked like it was from the Belgium era. It had the kilometers to several interior Congolese cities that he was unfamiliar with. He decided to take a picture of it and wondered where the sign had originally been posted. Another strange piece was a motorcycle engine propped up next to a dilapidated bike. He leaned over to examine it, wiped the dust off the tank, and stepped back in surprise.

"Whoa! An Indian!"

It looked ancient. James wondered who it had belonged to and why it was there. It was clear that while the bike had its own motor, the separate engine belonged to it, too. He wondered if the second motor had been bought for parts to repair the original one. James decided that this needed to be documented also, and not just on paper. He pulled his cell phone out and took several shots of the bike along with closeups of serial numbers. He intended to look it up on the internet later and ask Kongolo some discrete questions.

James had just about finished his tour of the depot when a metal ring on the floor caught his attention.

It was in the northwest corner of the room. At first, it just appeared as if it were simply laying there, but when James went to pick it up, he found that it was attached to a solid piece of wood, most likely ebony. The dark color was a stark contrast to the hard, mud floor surrounding it. James was breathing heavily with intense excitement and curiosity as he positioned himself to heave on the ring and raise the trap door, but his action was suddenly interrupted.

"Hey, Pressman." James tried to sound casual as he gathered himself into an upright position.

"Having any luck, James?" his colleague asked, looking left and right and taking in the room. "Nobody ever comes in here. It's just an old storage room for junk."

"Yeah, so I've noticed. I really appreciate your suggesting that I take a look in here." James snickered with a hint of sarcasm.

Pressman smiled. "Find anything useful?"

"Nope. Just made a list of common things like hammers and screwdrivers. The only really interesting thing in here is this motorcycle," James said, moving in the direction of the Indian and attempting to draw Pressman's gaze away from the corner where the ring was.

"What's so special about an old motorcycle?"

"It's not just any old motorcycle; it's an Indian. I would think it would be worth something to a collector. Have a look." James gestured toward the bike.

"Motorcycles aren't my thing," Pressman said. "I can't learn any more by getting closer, but it is intriguing that a collector's piece would be shoved in this shed." He took a step back toward the door. "Well, if you're okay, I'll leave you to your work. But I wouldn't linger too long. This place has got to be a hotbed for scorpions or even snakes. Either would be a nasty encounter."

James laughed. "Again... thanks for suggesting I come in the first place."

"Anytime. That's what friends are for." Pressman turned around, leaving James to wonder if his "friend's" appearance was accidental or planned. He stood there for a full minute contemplating his showing up just as he was about to lift that trap door. He concluded that a coincidence was unlikely. And that idea unnerved him.

He glanced out at Pressman's retreating figure and decided to risk giving the ring a tug. He strode back over, yanked with all his might, and watched as the floor pulled up on a nearly hidden hinge. Inside a few wooden steps led down to a narrow passage. He knew that he desperately wanted to explore the chamber, but he also knew that his flashlight was back in his room.

James thought that he would like to have a real friend watching his back while he was down there. He'd have to arrange to get Kongolo in on this at another time, and soon. He replaced the flooring, positioned a few gas cans over it, closed the back window, and slipped out the front door, shutting it securely. He had even more to think about than before his outing to the depot. He walked back to his room with a short stop to pound some water. He locked himself in and sat down in front of the fan to think.

Chapter 16

James loved to think on paper. Typically, he would use large sheets, pencils, and a straight edge to plot and map the thoughts flowing through his mind. But today, he paused to worry about who would find his musings. How could he protect his suspicions while still being fully able to express himself and tackle his mounting problems? He realized that he would need to create a simple code or cipher. These were part of every Special Forces soldier's training, and with his background in communication, he was better than most. But he also realized that this international community of responders and reporters were smart. Probably smarter than his ability to code without being easily hacked by an ambitious information seeker.

He opened his laptop to peruse the most common codes and encryption templates. He wanted something that would be easy for him to create and remember, but personal enough to slow down anyone interested in what he had to say. He found a simple cipher wheel, wrote out a grid, and began working. It was nothing complex, and he knew that with a little curiosity and a bit of effort, any trained person could decipher it. But it was a good place to start and would at least act as a first tier of security. He decided to write out and memorize key words. These he would use repeatedly, and he wanted to not have to keep referring to his template.

James began his mind mapping with the number-corresponding word for Ebola at the top of the paper. In the middle, he placed the compound and a rough sketch of its buildings and dimensions. He then placed other words around the compound. The number word for lesula he wrote on the area where they were spotted that morning. He put the number equivalent for Congo at the bottom of the page. Simple words like prepositions and conjunctions he kept in their typical alphabet forms.

Soon, he felt comfortable with his growing map. He leaned back in his chair, looked at it from a different viewpoint, then stood up. He was groggy again despite his nap. He decided to tack the paper to his mosquito net with a clothes pin and think standing up with the fan directed straight at his back.

His mind returned to two irritating thoughts: the lesula and the trap door in the depot; not to mention Pressman's sudden appearance at the depot. Plus, there were the signs that indicated that he was not being truthful about the helicopter. James wrote out the number equivalent for suspect with Pressman's name next to it.

It was supper time and James' tee shirt was finally dry. So, he stood up, put the shirt back on, brushed his hair, and headed out the door to eat. The meal that night was spaghetti with meat sauce, another favorite with the international community. One of the chefs had even taken the time to make garlic bread out of some of the local baguettes. The meal was a hit, and the conversation around the table and room flowed freely despite the seriousness of their reason for being together.

Lucas and James finished about the same time. They nodded at each other before separating to grab writing things from their rooms. Both men were in the lounge within five minutes.

"So, tell me what's on your mind, Lucas. A new friend told me this morning that you would be the best source of information." Because everyone was still at supper and the room was empty, James felt secure in coaxing his new friend to speak freely.

Despite their privacy, Lucas leaned in close before starting. "This Ebola is serious stuff, and it goes way beyond just a lethal virus. Listen, there are two main things on my mind. One is a break in protocol I noticed that happened twice; the other is something I heard whispered in a language I wasn't supposed to understand."

"Tell me about the protocol concern," James encouraged.

"So, last week, I was coming out of the women's ward and preparing to walk into the children's. Every time up until that moment, when I had walked out of a ward, I was greeted by someone, also suited up, who would rinse me down with bleach. This safety measure was always used between wards and, of course, after we were done making our rounds for the day. But this time no one was there. I tried calling for help thinking that the normal nurse was just outside the door or preparing the solution. But no one answered. I decided that I needed to exit the wing altogether to look for the bleach myself or just move on to the next ward and hope the nurse would meet me there before entering, but no one was there either. I didn't know what to do, so I found a bottle of bleach in a small bathroom and merely rinsed off my gloves before continuing my rounds."

"When exactly did this happen?" James asked, making notes in shorthand. "And did you say it happened a second time?"

"Yes. The first time was last week on Wednesday, May 31st. The second time was just this past Sunday. I was forced again to find a bottle of bleach and wash my own gloves. There's danger in that. I touched the doorknob of that bathroom twice with non-sanitized hands. I could have inadvertently spread the virus in this way."

"Strange," James replied. "Just today one of my local security chiefs stated that the population in the village of Domiongo are worried that protocol isn't being followed; that their relatives are in more danger of dying here than in their own homes." James indicated that in his notebook and mentally promised himself to follow up and see if there was a connection between this event and the locals' concerns. "What was the second thing?"

"That has to do with a conversation I overheard in the response office. You know, the building just inside the front gates. I was emailing my boss at Samaritan's Purse about the breach in protocol, when I overheard two people talking through the open windows. They were speaking French, which I know a little. One was saying something about researching the virus on a type of monkey. I didn't know the word that they were using, so I quickly looked it up on my laptop. It was 'lesula.' I had never heard of any testing being done on animals, so I was really shocked. What do you think? Am I just being paranoid?"

"No. Not at all," James assured him. "Lucas, I saw something today that confirms your suspicions. I could tell you but don't want to put you at any more risk."

"Tell me." Lucas exclaimed. "I'm already at risk by walking into that clinic every day."

James let out a small chuckle before continuing. "On my hike today while doing a tour of the compound this morning with Katey and Facundo, we saw a troop of lesula way up in a tall bonyanga tree. They seemed unafraid to be so close to humans. That surprised us all. My worry is that these monkeys were used for research but escaped... or worse."

"What could be worse? Wait. You don't think that they were

released on purpose, do you?"

"I'm not saying anything at this point," James said. "I'll investigate the situation carefully, but I don't want you to share this theory with anyone, here or stateside. The less people who know our suspicions, the better. Can I get your word on this?"

"Of course. And I hope neither theory is a reality. The danger is there, but if the monkeys were released deliberately, that speaks of malicious intent. If that's the case, not only are we in danger, but the whole village or region, for that matter!"

James took copious notes while Lucas sat back deep in thought. Neither wished to speak openly any more about the lesula or the broken protocol. They agreed to keep their ears to the ground for any more tidbits. If nothing happened, they would meet again on Saturday afternoon.

James took one last trip to the WC, then returned to his room to lock himself in for the night. His first full day in Domiongo was more than he bargained for, and he needed time to debrief himself and unwind.

Chapter 17

Just as James locked his door, a notification came through that he had gotten an email from Julia. He strode over to his laptop and opened it to catch her message.

```
Hello Sweetheart!

Hope your first day was better than you
expected. Things here are fine. Silas
keeps asking when you'll return, and
Luke just seems a bit confused that
you are not walking through the door in
the evening. The weather is perfect!
Very typical of summers here, as you
know. I took the boys to the park
today and let them play in the creek
for an hour. It wore them out enough
for them both to take a good nap.

Keep me in the loop as you take on more
tangible issues. Don't forget to tell
me all about the people you meet. I'd
love to hear your take on them. You're
so good at reading personalities. I
miss you already. I can't believe that
this mission has no solid end date.
Take care of yourself. I love you!

Julia
```

James clicked the laptop shut. He decided he would respond after some time alone, but then quickly changed his mind.

```
Hey Babe,

Glad that you're keeping those boys
worn out. I think that will have to
be your survival strategy. Tire them
out each morning. Let them nap every
afternoon. That way you get some down
time. I have a favor to ask you. Can
you do some research on a reporter
named Victor Archer? He works with
Sky News out of London. His family is
very controlling, apparently because
he comes from old money. I'd like
more information on his background.
Could you do that for me? I'd rather
have the security of a cell phone
conversation but emailing the info
will probably be okay too. Text me
when you're ready for that chat.

Honestly, I'm already a bit worried
about this assignment. Some weird
things are going on, and I want to
get to the bottom of them without
raising any suspicion. Please connect
with all our friends, family, and
church members to join in prayer for
my safety and wisdom. Thanks.

I love you, Julia; very much!

Me
```

James wanted to do some thinking without being interrupted. He placed everything that he would need for the task inside the mosquito net, even his laptop. He gathered all his notes, notebooks pens, pencils, a water bottle, and a granola bar before once again positioning the fan inside the netting and turned it on. Leaving only the lamp on next to his bed, he settled into analytical mode.

I need to write out general duties for tomorrow, but at the top of the list is speaking with Katey about getting a team together to cut back those trees and organizing a trip to the village to look for razor wire. Hopefully, while I'm there, I can pick up some chatter regarding the concern over breaches in protocol.

James wrote his tasks down, often replacing key words with his simple code. He finished by calming his mind with the day's chapters of both Proverbs and Psalms, journaling, and praying for his family, himself, and for the safety of the staff working this crisis. These men and women were counting on him to do his job and do it well. That was a responsibility he took very seriously. He consumed the granola bar, drank some water, and did some focused breathing before clicking off the light. One last sigh as his head hit the pillow, and he was gone.

Chapter 18

As usual, morning came early for James, but this time he was glad about it. His clock said four as his mind was absorbing the crowing of a rooster not too far away. He sat up, rubbed his face thoroughly to wake up his brain, and checked the floor around his flipflops for critters. Climbing out of bed, he stretched out the kinks that his muscles felt after a night on a rather poor-quality foam mattress and immediately dropped to the floor for some pushups and burpees. He'd missed his workout routine back on base these past few days, and somehow his instinct told him that being in peak physical condition would come in handy on this mission.

James drank the rest of his water bottle and grabbed the things he needed for a shower. He both dreaded and looked forward to the chill of the water. His mind cringed, but it was also his mind that would most benefit from the coldness, knowing it created a dopamine boost.

Once again, he looked carefully around the compound as he stepped out of his room and locked the door. He was feeling wary of his companions on this mission. His gut told him things that he did not really want to acknowledge. The cool, damp, morning breeze gently fanned his face and lifted the few tufts of brown-blonde hair on the top of his head. Once he had started his teaching position, he had decided to wear his hair a little longer on the top but still kept it trimmed short on the sides and back. He rounded the corner of the press corps dorms and came up to the WC. His did his morning business and stepped into the shower room after carefully scrutinizing it for spiders.

The experience was great, both cleansing and invigorating. The cold water cleared his mind, almost shocking him into a more focused analytical state. What James had considered hopeless and scary the previous night, now seemed surmountable. He dried, dressed, and returned to his room to straighten his bed, organize his clothes, and prepare for his new morning routine in the cafeteria. He hoped to spend time in there focusing on God and His Word, as well as the day ahead.

Just as before, Victor was seated at the press table with his laptop open. The men exchanged a hearty good morning. James filled his cups with water and coffee and fixed some bread. He settled again in the corner to pursue some intentional effort at preparing his mind and body for the day.

His Bible reading and journaling routine had a decided pattern divided into three chapters. He read one from a gospel first, then skipped over to read a portion of Proverbs that corresponded with the day of the month and finished with a final one in the book of Psalms to guide his prayers. James did these three through consecutively and had done so for years. From time to time, on a weekend, he would read an entire epistle in one sitting just to stay fresh on his doctrine.

Being exactly a week into the month of June, when he got to Proverbs, he read through chapter seven which was about Solomon warning his son against the dangers of the seductive woman. James had always regarded this chapter as something he really didn't need. Because he'd loved Julia since they were students in high school, he never looked twice at any other woman in the thirteen years that they were apart, and he had eyes for only her since they were married six years prior. But, for some reason, on that particular morning, he decided to give the instruction more credence. This mission presented the first opportunity in years to mix with potentially "strange" women. As he read, he strengthened the resolve to continue guarding his heart.

James focused on the contrast between the perverse woman and wisdom, which was the theme in the beginning of the chapter. Wisdom stood out as the most protective female companion that a man could have. James knew that he would need to cling to that in order to survive this mission both safe and untainted. He underlined several notes to himself so that he could meditate on this thought in the days ahead.

Once James was finished and had devoured his first breakfast, he got up to chat for a few minutes with Victor, who asked more questions about how James and Julia had met and about his boys. James always took pride in telling his love story with Julia and enjoyed the eager audience. Victor did not speak much of himself, and James wondered if he thought that he'd shared too much yesterday. He was eager to hear from Julia on this man's backstory.

Other team members began to trickle in. James said goodbye to Victor and headed up to fill his plate with the main entrée: cornmeal mush, cinnamon toast, and boiled eggs. He took plenty of everything. Fixing his porridge with butter, sugar, cream, and peanut butter, he considered how vital fat and protein were to his brain, and he knew he would definitely need it for this mission. Others followed his preparations and soon the whole room was exclaiming how the mush tasted like Peanut Butter Captain Crunch.

After breakfast, James texted Facundo and Katey to bring their units to the lounge for their first all-staff meeting, which was set for ten o'clock. Everyone was eager to begin work under James' guidance.

Chapter 19

The morning meeting with Facundo, Katey, and their respective units went better than James anticipated. Both the Uruguay and the Congo groups were eager to do whatever necessary to prevent the spread of the disease.

Katey organized his men to cut back the trees that morning. They found the appropriate tools in the shed to get the job done. Both units expressed relief to have James there to oversee the security of the mission. He ended by offering a prayer for their discernment, which all the men thoroughly appreciated. They recognized the seriousness of their job and the need for divine wisdom.

After everyone went off to their specific duties, James pulled Katey aside. "Hey, I'd like to go into the village of Domiongo today. Can you take me? I want to try to locate that razor wire. And if I can gain any intel from village leaders or whoever is willing to share about the concerns over medical protocol, that would be a huge bonus. Do you have time right after lunch?"

"Yes. That is a good time," Katey agreed. "I will meet you at the front gate with my brother who has a taxi. Do you have American dollars? That's how he prefers to be paid if it is possible."

"I do," James responded. "I brought enough money in small bills like fives and tens for situations like that. Sometimes money is the best form of security."

The men agreed on a time and parted ways. James went back to his room to check emails and look over the notes he took during his first security team meeting. He took the time to translate important parts into code. Once things were organized, he thought he'd like to buy a lockable box for storing some of his notes and considered taking extra cash for that purpose when he went to town.

After a simple lunch of tomato soup and grilled cheese sandwiches, James changed into his flipflops and headed down the path toward the front gate. As he passed the clinic, he heard the cries of family members just outside being informed that their loved one had died. The Congolese mourned differently than westerners, and their soul-wrenching wailing touched James at his core. Until that moment, he had not really understood how valuable his task was on a personal level. Slowing down the depths of human agony and pain was worth the risk.

He sighed, prayed, and shed a tear or two before he arrived at the gate. Katey was admitted just as James was approaching the UN sentinel on duty who was a friend of Facundo that he had met that morning in his first meeting. "Hello, Andreas. How are you?"

The sentinel nodded toward the sound as he responded. "Well, I've been better."

"I know," James replied. "Not something you want to hear on a daily basis."

"Yes. Truly, it is very difficult to stand here today and listen to this weeping. I am very sad in my heart for this," Andreas revealed, showing the depths of his own raw emotions with a slowly exhaled breath.

"Hello, Katey." James greeted as the third man approached. "Did you get that taxi? I'm ready if you are."

"It is just here," Katey gestured. "Come, I must first introduce you to my brother, Paul. He is honored to meet you and to drive a mundele into the village. Although the north end is not far, the main market is in Centreville." The group walked over to the young man and introductions were made. They got into the taxi, which was nothing more than a small, old Volkswagon Golf.

"Mbote, Paul! I would shake your hand, but we are attempting to not spread the virus."

"Thank you, sir." Paul said. "This is as close as I want to be to it. Ebola is a work of the devil, I believe. Where are we taking you? My brother says you need razor wire."

Katey piped up. "Do any of the Lebanese shop owners have this, Paul?"

"I am not sure."

"Also, James is seeking information. He has questions about some sensitive matters. Who can we trust to give him answers?"

"Amin, I believe, is the man you want," Paul responded. "He knows much about the village. His shop is on the main road that runs between Ilebo and Kananga, right at the front of the Marche Centre. I will take you there first. If he does not have razor wire, he will know who does. We will go there straight away."

They passed the north end of the town, mostly a residential quarter with mud and stick huts and thatched roofs. The houses became slightly more sophisticated as they drew closer to Centreville. In the middle of town was a small section of older, cement-brick Belgian structures that had been built in the 1950's and '60's. Most were completely walled in, many with armed guards outside the gates. The neighborhood soon gave way to the area near the main market.

Paul parked the car and paid a young man to watch it for him. The three walked into a store with rebar over the windows that was painted in gaudy colors. The name over the door was Walli-mart, which made James snicker. Once inside, he realized that the store was bigger than it had originally appeared. A thirty-something Lebanese man rose from the stool behind the counter to greet his guests. He seemed honed-in on meeting the mundele and finding out why he was in his store.

"Greetings. My name is Amin. Are you American?" He stuck out a hand to shake with James, who waved both of his in front of him.

"I'm very sorry. I am working with the international response team addressing the outbreak. We have a protocol of not greeting that way. And, yes, I am American. My name is James. I have been assigned to head up security, which is why I'm here. I need some razor wire."

While he waited for Amin to respond, James took a moment to observe the whole store. He was immediately struck by the intense heat and stuffiness. Although a fan was doing its best to push around the heavy air, James' shirt clung to his skin with the humidity. His nose was also attacked by a variety of odors. Some pleasant, others not so much. Bar soap, shampoo, and laundry soap caught his attention and turned his head in that direction. Women's cloths lined the back wall behind the counter. Machetes and knives lined the right wall, while food items could be found to the left.

"Hmm. Razor wire? And what do you need to secure with it?"

"We are currently shoring things up around the response compound," James informed him. "One area seems a bit inadequate. I would like to install it on top of the barrier there."

"I see. Yes. Well, I myself do not carry it. If you wanted to get it brand new, I believe that it must ordered from Kinshasa and flown up here. However, there might be another option. I know that a man on the other side of town began to build his, how do you say, his dream home? He brought many materials here for this project, but he ran out of money, and it came to a stop. One thing he has is razor wire. He may be willing to take American dollars for it. Shall I call him and ask?"

"Sounds perfect. Do you know how much he has? How many meters?" James turned to confer with Katey on the measurement needed to complete the back fence.

"The whole clearing is, I believe, about three hundred meters," Katey said. "But the fence is a bit smaller."

Amin was already on the phone speaking with his acquaintance. He heard the quote of three hundred meters and conveyed it to the man on the other end of the line. In a moment the conversation was finished, leaving Amin smiling.

"Good news, James. This man purchased a great amount of razor wire. He says he has more than five hundred meters. He can bring it here so that you can inspect it. He will sell it for the price he paid including shipping. Do you have the money with you? He can arrive in about twenty minutes."

"Depends on the amount," James responded. "I didn't bring much cash with me, but I believe that the transaction can be made at the compound, or I can return and be back here in a short while with it. What do you think?"

"Let us inspect the quality of the wire first," Amin suggested. "Then we can make our decision." He glanced around the store, then pulled James to one side near the counter. Katey followed. Paul walked out front to wait for the razor wire owner. "James, I need to discuss something with you. Do you mind if I bring up the outbreak? There are many questions being asked in town, especially here in the market."

"Sure. What's on your mind," James encouraged, knowing information was vital for security.

"People are very worried, very agitated. I am fearful for myself and my children to be here during this virus. People are saying that proper safety protocol is not being followed in the clinic part of the hospital. Relatives are saying that the doctors are not sanitizing between visits to the various patients. Is this true?"

"I cannot really speak openly about this," James began, "as there is an ongoing investigation. Let me only say that this is the third time that I have heard this, and I've only been in the country for a few days. I'm also worried. You must know that I'm going to do my best to get to the bottom of it. I've been chosen because I know my job well and understand the seriousness of this situation. Please do me a favor, though. Spread the word that I am here and plan to do the best I can to secure the compound and outbreak. Will you do this?"

"Yes," Amin agreed. "I understand the importance of keeping the population calm. If they get very agitated, they may riot. I overheard someone suggest that the other day."

"Not good news," James admitted.

"I agree. My wife and children live here with me. I do not want any risk of them getting sick or being in the middle of a riot. A mob of angry people is nearly impossible to control. Another threat that I have heard is that family members want to take their sick relatives by force from the clinic compound. Some want to flee to another region. Others desire to bring their sick to a local witch doctor. This must not happen."

"It can't," James stated matter-of-factly. "Neither of those threats will keep the disease contained. Katey, what can be done on your end to prevent the village from getting out of control?"

Katey pondered James' question for a second.

James pushed, "We need to keep the population calm. If they panic and leave, the virus could spread to other areas of the country."

"I believe that we need to prove to the people that protocol is in place," Katey said after some consideration. "Although we doubt that things are being done exactly right, overall, the proper steps are being taken to keep things very safe."

"What do you suggest?" Amin asked.

"I think that we should take a few chiefs from the village on a tour of the compound," Katey offered. "Let them meet the doctors. Let them see how their families are being treated. If the chiefs are convinced, then they will convey this to the people."

"Katey has a fine idea," Amin affirmed as James nodded his approval. "But I do believe that this must be done soon. If the village is confident about the safety of the response, they will not riot or use force to remove their relatives."

The conversation ended abruptly as the man with the razor wire approached the store.

The group moved outside to meet him.

"Hi. I'm James Worthy." James greeted the man by waving his hands. "What's your name?"

Katey interpreted the question and turned to introduce the man to James. "This is David Lutete. He has the razor wire in the back of this man's taxi. Come look."

They stepped over to the open Volkswagon bus door. The vehicle appeared to be ancient but was still running well. James inspected the wire. There seemed to be a sufficient amount for the job. Although it was rusty in spots, it appeared to be strong enough to protect the compound.

"This looks good. How much does he want for it?" James asked, turning to Katey. Once again Katey translated. This process took longer since it appeared that the men were bartering over the price.

James expected it to be higher here than it was in the states, especially because of the extra shipping costs.

"David says that he will sell it to you," Katey translated, "for three hundred American dollars. I believe that this is a little high, but since it is convenient to have it already here, I think it is worth it."

James agreed to the price. He asked Katey to explain that the men would need to follow them back to the compound so he could get the money. He asked if they would be willing to wait outside the gate. The men gave their consent.

James said goodbye to Amin. They exchanged cell numbers and promised to keep in touch over any developments. The van followed their smaller vehicle back to the compound where James was admitted. Katey stayed outside the gate to wait for James to return. It took longer than expected as tracking down Pressman and getting the cash proved difficult.

Once the transaction was finally made, James located a dilapidated pushcart and hauled the razor wire to the shed. He had already arranged for Katey to have men on the compound by eight the next morning to work on installing it and cutting back more trees.

James spent the rest of the afternoon in his room and then enjoyed a simple supper with his new colleagues. The conversation was pleasant despite the circumstances of their being together. Stories about how they met their wives and the antics of their kids made the hours pass quickly.

James was glad to be finished with another day and looked forward to resting and refreshing his mind. It would be followed by a new start.

Chapter 20

Again, James was up early. Ten minutes till four. He was getting into a great morning routine, and he loved it. He made his bed, grabbed his shower things, and opened the door to his room. He felt invigorated by the wind, one of his favorite parts of nature. Allowing the gentle, damp breeze to caress his cheeks and lift his hair, he breathed in deeply, and then out slowly. He did this several times, filling his brain with oxygen and calming his entire body. Headed around the corner of the press dormitory on his way to the shower, he nearly ran straight into a woman leaving the same area but going in the opposite direction. She was dressed only in a long towel, her hair wrapped in a smaller one.

James mumbled an apology, but the woman just gave him a quick, hard-to-read look. She brushed past him without a word and continued around the corner. James turned to watch her. For some reason, something about this woman set off alarm bells, but he couldn't figure out why. He had not seen her before in the few short days that he had been on the ground in Domiongo so he assumed she was relatively new to the response team. His sixth sense told him something was off, and experience had taught him to listen.

James pondered all of this as he stepped in to relish his icy-cold shower. While spitting the water from his mouth, a thought popped into his mind. He remembered the helicopter that he had heard the other night, the one that Pressman had so easily dismissed. This thought, once lodged in his mind, refused to let itself be ripped away. He wondered if that was how she had gotten there. But, if so, why hadn't he seen her before now? And why was Pressman being surreptitious about the whole event? Did he know something? Was he hiding something? If so, what?

James strode back to his room to email Julia and put together his journaling things. He decided to travel light this time and use the Bible app. on his phone instead of carrying his physical one. James was focused on discovering who this woman was and wondered if Victor had any answers. He pulled on an olive-green tee shirt and khaki shorts and slipped into his flipflops. At the entrance of the cafeteria door, he stopped to assess the room. The task was easy. Other than Kongolo and the main chef in the kitchen, only Victor was in the room. He said good morning as he went to prepare his breakfast.

James felt Victor's gaze follow him as he walked toward the drink and bread table. Wondering what it meant, as he downed two glasses of water and filled a third for sipping, he prepared his coffee and bread and returned to his table. He settled down to enjoy his first meal of the day and plunge into the reading and writing routine that he had come to so appreciate. This morning, however, he was distracted. While he understood that some might view his worries as unfounded, he had also spent the better part of a lifetime learning this survival skill of trusting his gut. He tried for several minutes to put the woman out of his mind and focus on what he was supposed to be doing, but he finally gave in and turned his attention to his new goal: finding out all he could about her identity and purpose for being there. Pulling out a pencil and a blank sheet of paper from the back of his journal, he decided to brainstorm and then mind-map what it was that was bothering him. His years of mixed military and Christian life experience had caused James to accept that God was often in the distraction business, using a disturbing thought to get on the right way of thinking about something.

He began by writing himself questions. What was her name? Why was she here? How did she get transported to the interior of the Congo? And where had she been until her sudden appearance this morning? He used his code to write his ruffled feeling and thoughts.

With the questions extracted from his mind and moved to a piece of paper, James felt the weight of worry lift. He took one more bite of his peanut butter bread and then headed over to chat with Victor.

"How're you doing? Getting enough rest on this assignment?"

Victor shrugged. "I'm okay. I have a lifelong habit of going to bed early and get up early, but I get by. You?"

"About the same," James answered. He paused before jumping right to what was on his mind. "I need to run something past you because I have an obligation as security head to know as much as possible. I saw a new face this morning on my way to the shower. A woman, probably in her mid-thirties, was just coming from there. I can't describe much about her since she was wrapped up in towels. Do you know who that might be? I'm not sure why I don't remember seeing her during the first few days here."

Victor hesitated for a split-second, looked at the floor, then lifted his gaze once again. "I can't be positive. You say that you saw her only this morning? Pressman will be in here in an hour; maybe you should ask him when he comes in."

"Well," James said flatly, "I was asking you. I thought that as a reporter you'd be up on everything going on here." He rose to leave when Victor placed a mildly restraining hand on his right forearm.

"Wait." Victor dropped his volume. "I really don't know who she is, but I do know that an extra reporter was due to show up this week. Since I'm the unofficial head of the media for this mission, Pressman came to me on Sunday before you arrived and said to expect someone new. He didn't give any details: no name, no organization, no description. Maybe my mind is on hyperdrive, but I feel like he wasn't sharing everything that he knew." Victor glanced around the room, clearly unnerved by the conversation. "Let's exchange cell information so that I can text you with anything else I learn."

James thanked him for being forthcoming, punched his contact information into his phone, and dismissed himself to go chat with Kongolo, who he had just seen come out of the kitchen.

Unfortunately, Kongolo could only spare a minute and had no inside information on the woman. He said he would keep his ears perked for any gossip to pass along.

James had to be satisfied with the little he had to go on. He returned to his chair, his coffee, and his bread. Focusing his mind with a Psalm and a prayer, he scribbled a portion of Proverbs 3:5 on the top of the brainstorming paper: *do not lean on your own understanding*. He affirmed with himself and God to not rely solely on his own training and experience. He needed divine assistance on this task.

The rest of the day passed without any sight of the newcomer. Breakfast with his colleagues went off without a hitch. Morning was spent organizing the crews that were cutting back the trees and attaching the razor wire to the top of the north wall and fence. Lunch, too, was nothing to mention. James spent several hours in his room achieving a short siesta, an email to Fitzpatrick, and pondering his various duties and the information that he had already gathered. He

He glanced at his watch and was shocked to realize that it was nearly suppertime. Where had the day gone?

Just as James was about to head over to supper, he received two texts, both of which seemed a bit cryptic. The first one was from Victor.

> Just saw her for the first time. Did not get to speak. Saw her talking with Pressman near the cafeteria door before she walked around back.

The second was from Lucas.

> It happened again. Not sure what to make of this break in safety standards. I asked another doctor from WHO if they knew what was going on. They acted unaware of anything. Almost unconcerned.

James responded to both with simple answers. He hoped to get a chance to speak to the men in person. Brushing his hair, he got himself ready for supper and headed out the door to the cafeteria.

Before entering, James paused for just a second, by habit, to scan the room. It was only half full, but he had noticed that several other team members were just leaving to walk over. He passed the press table and caught Victor's eye. Victor nodded his head a fraction of an inch toward the food window. James followed his gesture and realized that the mysterious woman was there. In an instant, he decided on a direct approach. Striding up to her, he noticed that she was taller than average, estimating her height at about five feet, eight inches. He stepped up to grab his pre-filled plate.

"Hello. I'm James Worthy, head of the security team for this assignment. Sorry for nearly running into you this morning. I haven't seen you around before. Can I get some information from you? Like your name, when you arrived, what your role is here?" James tried to sound casual and yet authoritative.

The woman turned her steel-gray eyes toward him and took in his face and physique in one quick glance. She permitted a glint of admiration to spark before she answered. "My name is J.P. Walker. I'm a reporter with the Times. Just arrived late yesterday. Now, if you'll excuse me, I'm heading over to the press table to get to know my colleagues."

Without giving James an opportunity to respond, she walked back to her table and sat just to the left of Victor. James observed her as she leaned in toward him and in a rather intimate gesture, placing her perfectly manicured hand gently on Victor's arm as she whispered something. She sat back and smiled, but he thought that Victor seemed shocked by the contents of her comment. James downed two waters before filling his glass for a third time. Again, he chose sweet, creamy tea and headed back to his typical table in the corner where Lucas was sitting.

Chapter 21

Instead of being satisfied after meeting J.P. Walker, James was even more disturbed. Deciding to put the woman out of his mind and focus on his concerns about the safety standards, he asked Lucas several pointed questions about who was supposed to be sanitizing him between patients and whether he had ever tracked them down to ask why they had left their post. Lucas did not have any information that calmed James' worries.

"Have you spoken to your American colleagues about this breach in protocol?" James asked. "Or, have any of the others shared similar scenarios?"

"I actually only asked that one WHO doctor," Lucas answered. "I have not asked any of my team members from the states. I'm not sure how to go about it without gaining unwanted attention. If someone is deliberately trying to sabotage this operation, why would I be the easy target for pulling this protocol stunt?" Lucas was visibly shaken. "I don't like it one bit. I have a family, James. I really want to be around to watch my kids grow up."

"I'm totally with you, Lucas. We're in the same boat. Let me make the inquiries. You just do your job. Keep your nose clean. Fly under the radar. I need someone that I can trust on the inside of that clinic. Looks like it's going to be you. I appreciate your text. Keep up that kind of communication any time you have a concern."

The men allowed their conversation to drift toward general topics as the table filled up, but both felt the gravity of the situation. Several times throughout the meal they exchanged meaningful glances. When dinner was over, the group separated to their rooms for the evening to rest and refocus for the next day. Upon returning to his, James noticed that he had received a message from Julia. He plopped on his chair in front of his laptop and opened his emails.

He read the subject line first:

```
Long Family History

Hello James, hope you're doing ok! I
can't believe that you've been gone
less than a week. Seems like forever.
The boys miss you and ask about you
twenty times a day.

I did some research on Victor Archer's
family. There were a ton of articles,
but they all pretty much said the
same things. Victor is the youngest
of the heirs to his family's vast
fortune. Seems like they have been
building their wealth for the last
seven hundred years or more from all
```

I've read. They were early in the business of loaning money.

Initially everything started way back during the Middle Ages when they often financed pilgrimages to the Holy Land for wealthy landowners. They also set up a system of credit with hostels between Europe and the Middle East along the journey. From then until now, they have been involved in international banking and investments.

The information on their personal lives was a bit more rote and rather obscure. I mean, genealogies were available, but the names seemed to repeat themselves. They don't appear to be royalty at all, but rather supporters financially of the royals throughout Europe over the centuries. You were also right about Victor's being single. He's considered the most eligible bachelor on the planet, but some tabloids hinted that he was expected to marry someone that his family approved of.

I'm sorry that I couldn't dig up anything more specific. I actually feel sorry for him. I can't imagine being subservient to the wishes of my family when it came to matters of the heart. But I did find out that Victor is a bit of a rebel. Instead of going into the family business, he had branched out into environmentalism and reporting on anything related to nature. He's been with Sky News for more than ten years.

```
I don't have much else. Are you staying
safe, I hope? Answer as quickly as
you can.

I love you, honey.

Me
```

James immediately plunked out a quick thank you email for her research. He missed her and said it as profusely as an email would allow. He sent virtual hugs to the boys and clicked his laptop shut.

He looked around his room. It was not yet dark outside, but it would be soon. James had noticed that Congo had a very short dusk and dawn and figured it had something to do with being so close to the equator. He knew that he could head to bed as soon as it was dark, which was less than an hour away, and he enjoyed the time to himself, especially when he had a lot of thinking to do. Being awake when most were asleep afforded him the solitude he appreciated.

After one last trip to the bathroom, he tucked into his room and pulled out his journal and the notes that he started the other morning on Proverbs seven. Opening his Bible, he reviewed the description of the seductive woman in chapter two. Although he had no indication, his gut was telling him to be careful; he worried that he might be facing a new enemy. Or at least one that was new to him. His enemies had always been male, but there was something about J.P. Walker that seriously disturbed him.

James was secure in the depth and history of his love for Julia, having never looked twice at any other female since his teen years. He also knew the strength of his love for God. But after an honest assessment of himself and an open acknowledgement of how even the mightiest have fallen, James took time to fortify himself, his heart, and his mind. King David, a deep lover of God, was not impervious to the temptations that assaulted him through Bathsheba. He hated to see himself as weak as David, but to assume that he was stronger would be foolish. Besides, this newcomer had given him an admiring glance, if only just for a second. His normally controlled ego whispered to his pride, prompting him to brush off a thought of being handsome enough to earn that look.

Suddenly, he felt that he needed reinforcement. He picked up his phone and texted his friend Caleb. They had met in basic training nearly nineteen years ago. Caleb was currently stationed in Hawaii with his family. The time difference would be great, but he knew he needed his friend. He asked Caleb to pray for him on this assignment in Congo and inquired as to whether or not he still dabbled with his ham radio.

Immediately, Caleb responded with an assurance of prayer along with his handle and frequency. James memorized the information and replied that he would connect with him by radio or burner cell in the next day or two, but he would text a heads up before doing so.

James felt so much more at ease after contacting his trusted friend, knowing Caleb would do anything in his power to assist him. He brushed away that nagging thought of deserving JP's appreciation and prepped his mosquito net and fan. He continued getting ready for bed by placing his flashlight, journal, pen, and water bottle inside the net, plugging his phone into the charger, and tucking the net around it near his pillow.

Within a few minutes, he fell into a deep sleep. The hours ticked by, but he was suddenly awakened by an unsettling feeling. Just as before, he could sense someone at the screened window behind him. James barely changed the angle of his head and was still able to catch a glimpse of the figure who appeared to be studying his room. He could hardly make out the entire face, but the moon was bright that night, helping to illuminate the profile.

James was certain that the face was not Congolese. It was rather lighter skinned making it probable that this was a westerner. He held his breath and remained motionless. Taking a moment to continue his observations before ultimately deciding to confront the peeping Tom, James gently placed his hand around his flashlight and felt for the switch. Quickly sitting up, he shined the beam directly into the face of the person outside the window. Immediately they raised their hand, covered their face, and turned away so quickly that James was unable to notice much, but not so quickly that he didn't catch the distinctive cleft in the chin. He recognized the gait as masculine and estimated the person to be approximately six feet tall. The figure quickly retreated around the side of the building nearer to the press dorms.

Deciding to pursue, James quickly grabbed shorts, pulled them on, and stepped into his flipflops. Opening the front door, he saw the man running around the side of the dorms toward the WC and showers. Faster than he'd ever run in sandals, James rounded the corner expecting the man to be a few steps in front of him. To his surprise, no one was in sight, but just beyond the bath area, James could hear branches snapping as the man ran into the woods on the northeast side of the compound. He continued to pursue but suddenly stopped. There were no more audible clues. The movement had ceased.

James stood near a tree hoping to mask his location. He switched off his flashlight, remained still, listened, and peered into the darkness in the direction of the once fleeing man. He could detect nothing. He had either vanished or was willing to stay put and wait James out. The dim light coming from the distant cafeteria filtered around that side of the dorm. James also waited. Waited for his eyes to adjust to the darkness. Waited for the man to sneeze or pant or do something. Anything. Looking forward, he carefully scanned the area without moving his head, hoping to catch a glint of something shiny on the man, like a watch face, a piece of jewlery, or some identifying mark.

He stood there for more than twenty minutes without seeing a thing, desperately wanting to look at his own watch. He had no idea what time it was but decided to give up, go back to his room, and assess the information he had gained.

Once James was out of sight, the mysterious figure moved from his cramped position just enough to open his phone. He typed in a name and sent the following text:

> Close call tonight. This guy sleeps light. Chased. Barely escaped. Going to lay low for a few days. Contact if you have questions.

The man sent the message, then immediately deleted it. He made his way to the gate that led to the village, let himself out, then disappeared into the night.

Chapter 22

James looked around the courtyard of the compound before going in to his room. No one was moving that he could tell. Once inside, he clicked the lock shut and checked the time. It was ten minutes till four. Time to be starting his day. He made his bed, grabbed his shower things, and began his new favorite freezing routine.

He dressed, brushed his hair and teeth, and prepared his journaling and quiet time things. It was only a few minutes after four, but he decided to head to the cafeteria for breakfast anyway. When he got there, he discovered he was the first one up besides the kitchen staff. He plopped his things down on the table in his typical spot in the back of the room, facing away from the wall as usual. He said hello to the men in the kitchen and asked the chef if he could have a few minutes with Kongolo.

James drank his water and prepared coffee for himself, tea for Kongolo, and bread for both of them. Once seated, he lowered his voice. "Kongolo, I need your help. . I know you're very observant. I'm looking for someone. Last night, I saw a man peering in my bedroom window for a second time. He was a mundele, about your height. He has a cleft here," James stopped and pointed to his chin before continuing. "I haven't seen this man before. Can you think of who it might be?"

Kongolo pondered James' description. "Was he slimmer? More like me?"

"He's not as broad as I am," James answered. "I would say thinner and lanky. "

"What time was it when you saw him?"

"It was about three-twenty when I woke up and realized that I was being watched. I must not have been sleeping very heavily. Maybe a twig broke or something," James said.

"Was there anything different between the two events?" Kongolo asked.

"Yeah, actually. The first night I never saw the person. I only noticed both flipflop and boot prints near my window. But this time I actually pursued the man around the press dorms. He disappeared into the forest behind the WC area. Then I lost him. I'm sure that he stopped and waited for me to give up, which I eventually did." James paused for a second. "Someone's coming in, so I'd better stop. I want you to contact me if you see anyone like I described. Let me put my cell number in your phone. Put yours into mine."

The men exchanged phones and entered their information. Kongolo finished his tea and bread in silence and returned to the kitchen. Only then did James realize that the person entering was Victor. He was happy about that and even happier that it was not J.P. Walker. James refilled his coffee, said good morning to his new friend, and returned to his chair to read his Bible and journal.

After he finished, he made an extensive to-do list. The first item on the agenda was to take a tour of the perimeter again to see how the trees looked, as well as the razor wire. Then he needed to call Katey to ask about a two-way radio in the village or a place to buy a cheap cell phone. He also noted to reinforce his mind against what he fully anticipated from more encounters with J.P. Finally, he decided he wanted to get to know Victor better. Oddly, he believed it was possible that their relationship could be important to his mission. With Proverbs seven in his mind, and the email from Julia, James rose to spend a few minutes with him before any others arrived for breakfast.

"Hey, you awake enough for a chat?"

"Sure. Have a seat. How're things going with your assignment?"

"Umm, pretty good, I think," James said. "Just getting started. We had men cutting back trees yesterday to prevent people from climbing over the wall from the street side."

"Good first step."

"Yep. Also found some rusty but still sharp razor wire in town the other day. That was supposed to be installed yesterday. On my list for today is to take a second tour of the compound perimeter to see the progress. Once I feel that the barrier wall is secure, I'll be able to rest better tonight."

"A tour sounds right up my alley. Mind if I join you? I mostly wait all morning to hear reports from the clinicians and then write in the afternoon. A walk around the compound would be a nice change of pace."

"Sounds fine to me," James said. "I'll probably be ready around nine. Can I meet you by the front gate a few minutes after that?"

"I'll be there." Victor affirmed. "So, did you look me up on social media yet? I've quite the high-profile life."

"I actually had someone else do it for me, but yes, I did read about your background and family. I can see why you feel so obligated to them. They have an awful a lot to protect."

Victor chuckled. "So, you had someone else do the research, ehh? I like you already."

James laughed with him before continuing, "Several articles mentioned that you're passionate about the environment. What's your favorite cause?"

"What exactly do you mean?" asked Victor, wanting clarification. "Like a specific issue I focus on?"

"Sure. Like the dwindling oceans? Or the diminishing rainforests? The bizarre weather patterns? What gets you most fired up?"

"Is 'all of the above' an acceptable answer?" he responded with a shrug.

"Of course," James chuckled.

"I've done a bunch of research, both in the classroom and out in the real world, so to speak. I really want to help people realize what they can do rather than what they can't do."

"Good positive position," James said.

"Exactly," Victor returned. "No one likes to be told which car to drive or that they should take public transportation, or which water bottle company is doing the best job of fostering sustainability. But everyone can do something to contribute to the long-term care of the planet. Do you consider yourself as an environmentalist, James?"

"Probably not in the way you think. I know that my worldview may be archaic to many, but I take my policy way back to the beginning, when Adam was told to be a good steward of the garden in which he was brought to life."

"A Biblicist?" Victor charged.

"Yep," James admitted, shamelessly. "Adam was instructed to care for the earth and understand and dominate the animal kingdom. To this day, I believe that man's a steward, that our planet is a gift to us from God, and that we have an obligation to preserve and properly utilize the resources He's given us. Weird?"

"No. Well, not really," Victor said. "I believe we're using different words, but it seems like our goals are the same."

"I guess," James nodded.

"Some take environmental concerns almost to the point of Earth worship," Victor added. "I don't see myself in that category. Besides, the real issue comes down to sharing my beliefs in the clearest way possible. Taking care of the planet should be fun; young people should want to be involved in the diverse ways of protecting the planet for the future."

"Sounds like you have a solid grip on your goals," James said. "But did your decision to become a journalist spring from your desire to communicate the things that you are passionate about?"

"They did."

"Cool," James acknowledged. "Does your family support that?"

"My family's very traditional, focusing on their money for centuries, which in all fairness has worked well for them. But now, people are realizing that with this many people on the planet our resources won't last forever. Using up fossil fuel at our current rate will certainly drain that one quickly. Looking for more sustainable energy sources will become necessary. Green should be more than just a marketing slogan; it needs to be at the center of research and industry. So, in many ways, my family's behind the times. They really need to see the importance of investing in new energy solutions."

"All good thoughts, but I have to change the subject drastically before anyone else comes in." James suddenly took a more serious tone. "How well do you know J.P. Walker? When she sat down next to you yesterday, it seemed as if you two were pretty tight."

Victor leaned close and nearly whispered, "I know her, but I can't talk about it here. Can we discuss this on our walk around the compound? I think it'll be easier to speak more openly then. Do you trust your Congolese counterpart?"

"I do trust Katey, and that sounds like an ideal time to chat."

"Great. Let's call it quits for now. People are starting to come in."

James got up from the table and went to get his coffee refilled and to pick up his real breakfast of pancakes. He fixed them with butter, peanut butter, and syrup, and returned to his table just as Lucas came in for breakfast. The two ate together in relative silence, both buried in thought about their respective roles in this mission which was becoming more unsettling by the minute.

Chapter 23

Around nine, James texted Victor that he was on his way toward the front gate. Victor saw him just as he was turning onto the main lane heading toward the entry of the compound.

"Hey, James, over here!" Victor called with a wave. James waited as Victor caught up. "I take it this is where we're starting. Just trying to take in the whole compound, I guess?"

"Yup. I want to really get to know this place well enough to even be able to navigate it in the dark. You never know when you'll need to chase someone through the forest." James chuckled as he motioned toward the dense foliage surrounding the main buildings.

"Wait," Victor started, "why the laugh? Did that already happen?"

"Hmm, let's just say it's already been an eventful day. I think I'll keep the details to myself, though. I don't want to worry you or make you accountable for any unnecessary information."

"Tell me," Victor begged. "James, you know my family has been keeping secrets for generations. Let me in on the good stuff. I promise

I won't report on anything you say without your permission."

James sighed before resigning himself to disclosing the recent concerning incidents. "Okay… Well, in the middle of the night I woke up to someone staring at me through my window. And it was actually the second time it happened."

"The second time?"

James continued, nodding. "I decided to chase him and followed him to the wooded area behind the press dorms. I lost him in the darkness, and he stopped moving, giving me nothing to go on. I paused and waited twenty minutes for him to sneeze or break a twig, but I got zilch. Finally, I just gave up and returned to my room. The first time I had no idea who it was. Didn't see any features. But this time I could tell that the man was tall, thin, and white. I also noticed that he had a pretty significant cleft in his chin. Doesn't sound like anyone you might know, does it?"

"No," Victor replied sincerely. "I haven't seen anyone here that matches that description. I'll keep my eyes open though."

"Thanks, Victor. I appreciate it."

"Don't mention it," he responded, continuing to ponder what James had told him. "Huh, you weren't kidding. You have had a long day already and it's barely nine." Victor slapped James on the shoulder.

"Tell me about it. Hey, there's Katey."

"Bonjour, messieurs! How are you both?" Katey greeted.

"We're fine, thanks. This is my friend Victor Archer. He's a reporter on the response team who asked to join us this morning. I'm looking forward to seeing the progress on the trees and razor wire."

"Yes. It is all finished. Follow me."

Katey led the way, and Victor and James walked side-by-side behind him for a while until the trail became too narrow. Katey paused where the trees were trimmed back to point out the difference. James admired the work, and Katey beamed.

"What's that?" Victor asked when they had walked up a little further. He pointed to something rather large lying just off the path to the right.

James and Katey paused to investigate, but what they saw sent chills down their spines. There, lying in the brush, was what appeared to be a dead lesula monkey.

Chapter 24

James, immediately on high alert, cautiously ventured closer and confirmed his suspicions. "Stay back," he ordered. "We don't know what caused this monkey to die. This is something that has to remain within our group until we can get some definitive answers."

James pulled out his phone and dialed Lucas' cell. "Hey, Lucas. Got a situation here."

"Uh-oh," came the reply on the other end. "That doesn't sound good."

"It's not," James agreed, matter-of-factly. "Do you have access to a solar-powered microscope?"

"Absolutely," Lucas replied. "And all the gear to go with it."

"Cool. I'm down the trail a ways with Victor and Katey, but I'll make my way back to the front gate. And if you can get your hands on something we could use to dispose of a small carcass, that would be great. Can you bring it all and meet me there in about five minutes?"

"Sure. I'll see you there." Lucas was full of questions but decided not to ask them.

James' face showed a mixture of relief and concern as he hung up.

"You don't believe this monkey died of Ebola, do you?" Victor asked.

"I do, actually. We need to stay clear of it until we have some answers. Lucas will be able to identify if Ebola is the killer. If that ends up being the case, then figuring out the best way to dispose of it will be our next trick."

Victor pulled out his phone and clicked on his recorder app. He began speaking notes and snapped several pictures. He knew that he had promised James to keep quiet, but he also knew that if he was cleared to share this information that he would need to be able to recall the date and location on the compound where the lesula was found. James left him with Katey and strode back to the front gate to meet Lucas.

His doctor friend walked up just as he was arriving. Both men looked around to see if they were being watched, then stepped onto the trail along the wall.

"What's up?" Lucas asked when they were out of earshot. "I hadn't yet started my rounds but getting my hands on this stuff and getting it packed up without being seen was a bit of work."

"Well, I appreciate you taking the risk, and here's the reason." James pointed to the dead lesula. "We were taking an inspection tour of the perimeter when we found this."

"Wow!" Lucas exclaimed. "This is a situation. Are you thinking what I am?" Lucas looked at the other men behind them.

"Both Victor and Katey have promised to keep this close," James assured. "Can you test to see if Ebola was the culprit?"

"Help me suit up."

Lucas pulled his full Personal Protective Equipment, informally known as PPE, from his duffel bag. James and Victor helped him into boots, gloves, and head gear. Once he was ready, and Katey had the bleach spray on standby, Lucas stepped up to the animal. He got the shock of his life when the monkey turned to stare at him with fever-tortured eyes.

"Whoa," Lucas exclaimed, stepping back. "I thought you guys said it was dead!" Although the animal was still alive, it was barely so. It clearly had no energy to flee, and the look it gave Lucas was that of a soon-to-be-departing soul.

"What should we do?" James asked. "Is there a way to access any of its bodily fluids to test for the virus?"

"Hmm. Do any of you see any vomit or blood nearby?" Lucas asked. "Anything?"

Katey, with his sharp eyes, found a bit of blood near the creature's mouth and pointed it out. Lucas grabbed a long stick, dipped the end in the fluid, and carefully transferred a smear onto the slide that Victor had handed him. James had the microscope set up on a close-by tree stump. Careful not to bump the sensitive equipment with his awkward suit, Lucas placed the slide in the tray. He peered carefully into the eye piece, then looked up grimly and nodded an affirmative. The men took a barely perceptible step back from the suffering animal.

"What should we do with it?" Victor inquired. "Do we report this?"

James just gave this question an unreadable look.

Victor continued, "Seems like we should, but to whom? We can't bury it alive, and we have no way to kill it without risking being infected ourselves."

"He will be dead very soon. Look at his breathing." Katey indicated the animal's gasping. "I say that we wait until he dies, then bury him here. But how he got infected, and why he was so close to this center of the virus, I find very troubling." As he was speaking, the animal's body sagged as it let out its last breath.

Lucas suggested that Victor and James dig as deep of a hole as they could, mostly using Katey's machete. He prepared the carcass to place in the small body bag that he had brought with him and placed it in the shallow grave. Lucas took the extra precaution of spraying bleach on everything that could possibly be contaminated before piling the dirt back over it. He carefully scattered leaves and twigs over the area, making it look as if nothing was there. Finally, he disinfected the spot where the animal had died.

James helped spray Lucas down and de-robe. The suit was draped over some bushes to dry while the men conferred about what should be done.

"Listen to me; I know this is scary," James said, "but at this point, we don't know who we can trust. As much as possible, this needs to be kept under wraps. We don't know how this monkey got infected, whether it was accidental or intentional."

Victor tried to protest but was stopped by James' raised hand.

"Let's keep it quiet. I need you particularly to restrain your natural instincts as a journalist. I'm beginning to suspect some awfully dangerous things." James spoke with authority. "Are we clear?"

"I respectfully disagree," Victor challenged. "If someone is testing on these animals, why wouldn't we all know about it? Lucas, are you involved in this type of research?"

"No. I'm not. And no one that I know personally is, but I did overhear something that made me suspicious. I've already shared this and other concerns with James earlier, which is fueling his skepticism."

Katey nodded his agreement.

Lucas continued, "I know you are worried, Victor, and I believe that you should be. I am. And James is right; we need to keep this quiet. Keep your notes, create your reports, but don't send anything just yet until we're sure of who to trust."

"Okay, okay," Victor assented. "But you all know that this event today has changed our perspectives and, with them, our mission. We need to be able to depend on each other's ability to keep a secret."

The men nodded in agreement.

Victor continued, "I know me. But I don't know you three well. All I ask is that from now on, you keep me in the loop. If my life is going to be risked reporting this horrific outbreak, I need to be fully confident that I can rely on the men asking for my secrecy."

James spoke up. "We need to have each other's backs. It may save our lives, the lives of our teammates, and the lives of the potential victims of this virus."

Katey and Lucas agreed readily, but Victor hesitated for a second. "Victor?"

"Okay, but I don't like it," he finally conceded.

In silence, the foursome walked slowly to the path leading to the back part of the cafeteria building. They decided to disperse at the clearing and to not speak obviously to each other for the rest of the day.

Upon returning to his dorm, Victor sat down in front of his laptop and just stared. He knew what James had asked of him, and he knew what his editor required. Trying to balance those two conflicting directives had given him pause.

He sighed and started to plunk away at the keyboard.

June 9, 2017

Today something very disturbing happened. I don't know what to make of it. I was on a hike around the perimeter of the compound property with the new security chief for the operation, James Worthy. It was meant to be a simple outing until a discovery changed everything.

There at our feet was a dying lesula monkey. The poor creature's eyes showed that he had only minutes to live. James called his friend who is a doctor working on the response team. The man arrived shortly with his full protective gear and equipment.

At James' request, some fluid from the animal was tested and confirmed what was suspected; it was infected with Ebola. Minutes later, the animal breathed his last.

With extreme caution, the monkey was properly buried. James made us swear to keep the information about the event to ourselves until he could further investigate how it became sick. He is suspicious of foul play. I'm placing this report in my draft and emailing you a copy. You are to share it with the editor only with my go ahead. Or if something happens to me.

I am very worried, my friend.

Victor

Victor pushed the send button and clicked the computer shut.

He didn't feel as if he had completely disregarded James' request by confiding in his friend with this information. He could only hope, if James found out, he'd see it the same way.

Chapter 25

Saturday came, and again James found himself up early with a lot on his mind. This was the day he had scheduled to get to the village to make a discreet call on that cheap burner phone he had purchased from Kongolo. He needed to pull someone from the outside into his corner about his worries concerning this assignment, and Caleb was the only one he knew that he could trust. Katey was going to meet him at the front gate at nine o'clock with Paul and his taxi to take him to make the call.

James loved being up early. Settled in his corner of the cafeteria, he completed his morning routine and fixed his bread and hot drinks. Already having added the Ebola-ridden lesula to his coded mind map the previous evening, James suspected that research was going on "under the table." He was further concerned that someone must have carelessly allowed the sick animal to escape its cage and that Lucas was being targeted for a break in protocol. They were very disturbing thoughts to ponder.

James specifically went looking for a verse near the end of Proverbs. He found it, chapter twenty-five, verse two: "It is a glory of God to conceal a thing: but the honor of kings is to search out a matter." This verse encouraged him to stay diligent in seeking the truth and he reminded himself that the God who conceals a thing also chooses to reveal mysteries as He did in the book of Daniel. James silently prayed that he, too, would be found worthy of such revelation. James already felt in over his head with this mission, knowing that he was ignorant about the minute details of the deadly virus and suspected that there was an element on the compound that could not be trusted. He even worried that Victor already knew too much. How could a reporter be asked not to report? And could he be trusted to not share what happened the day before?

James finished his breakfast in prayer. Other than the kitchen staff, he was the only one in the room which, at first, made him wonder where everyone was, but then he realized that it was his first Saturday on the base. Maybe sleeping in was common on the weekend. His suspicions were confirmed when, at ten 'till eight, people began to trickle in. Lucas ambled through the door looking more weighed down that he typically did. Picking up his breakfast tray, he stepped over to the drink table just as James approached the kitchen window.

"Good morning, Lucas. Hope you got some sleep last night."

"Some, but it wasn't great. I woke up a lot, thinking about

yesterday's event every time. You sleep okay?"

"I did. I knew I would be bothered by that as well, and I've found that getting things out of my mind and onto paper usually helps me to sleep better than if I don't, so I did quite a bit of journaling before going to bed. Listen, Lucas, don't worry about yesterday. Do what you came here to do. Let me be concerned about the issues."

"I'll try."

The two men finished the meal nearly in silence and almost nearly alone. Their normal mealtime mates came in very late. James excused himself to go back to his room and prepare for his trip to town.

He prepped a belt pack with Congo francs and small bills in American dollars. He had brought plenty of ones, fives, and tens with him from the states. Putting in lip balm, hand sanitizer, and some napkins, he then attached a small water bottle to the side. Lastly, he applied sunscreen liberally on his arms, face, and ear tips. He hated getting his ears burned. Shutting and locking his door, he began the walk toward the front gate.

"James," Victor called from behind to get his attention, "wait up."

"Hey. Missed you at early breakfast this morning. Doing okay?"

"Yup. I realized I forgot to answer a question you asked me on our walk yesterday." Victor waited until they were several hundred feet past the end of the medical dorms. "You wanted to know if I was familiar with J.P. Walker. The answer isn't exactly straightforward.

I've heard of her, but I'd never met her in person until this mission."

"Is she famous or something?"

"More like infamous. She comes from a family that's rather intertwined in global affairs. My family has done business with hers for more than a hundred years. Together, they've made millions, maybe even billions. But although our families are similar, by reputation she is very different from me. I have to warn you, she is a shrewd and dangerous woman. A happily married man should steer clear of her. She's been known to destroy many relationships."

"Got it."

"Let me take it further anyway. She used to maliciously ruin men's lives for sport, but I suspect she has since turned her skill set into employment. I believe someone at the top of the food chain uses her to manipulate lives for their advantage. Even when she doesn't succeed in her high-stakes game, she's still able to make them pay by spreading rumors. Please, just be cautious. Do not be seen alone with her."

"She seemed as if she knew you the other day by the way she was behaving. And whatever she whispered to you sure seemed to cause a disturbing reaction."

Victor paused. He looked down the pathway in front of him and sighed, "She simply told me that it would be a mistake to interfere with her. Like I said, I have never met the woman. But I know enough of her family, her fierce loyalty to them, and her corrupt name to know that she's to be avoided at any cost. If she attempts to go after you, I will do all I can to soften the blow."

James spoke in a grateful tone. "I so appreciate your concern. Listen, we're almost to the front gate. Head back before you arouse suspicion. This J.P. may already have paid eyes and ears in this place. Take care of yourself. I promise to keep you in the loop about any developments regarding her. I'll be sure to not willingly give her any ammunition to use against me."

James waved two hands at Victor, a typical Congolese gesture, turned and said good morning to the main gate sentinel, then walked outside to meet Katey and Paul. Victor had given him a lot to think about and another topic of conversation to discuss on his call. As James stepped into the Volkswagon Golf, he texted Caleb to expect contact within twenty minutes.

Chapter 26

"Mobte, Monsieur James," Paul greeted. He felt honored to be carrying a light-skinned mundele in his taxi, especially an American. It gave his service a bit of distinction in their small town. "How are you? Olamuki malumu?"

"I did wake up well," James replied. "Thank you for asking."

Katey, too, said his good morning.

"Where are we headed, men?" Paul asked.

"I need a secure place to make a phone call," James began to answer while turning his attention to Katey. "Did you find somewhere I could do that?"

"Yes," he quickly affirmed. "The man we purchased the razor wire from, David Lutete, is willing to set you up with what you need. As much as anyone, he desires to see our region free of this evil virus. He will be discreet with your business."

"Well, I'm grateful he's available. I hope you and Paul are willing to stand guard out front while I make the call."

"Of course, sir," Katey assured him. "We understand the need for privacy. Especially in your situation."

Paul drove the whole length of town on the main road that went from Ilebo to Kananga. David's house was clear in the southeast part of the village, in a neighborhood of newer, half-constructed homes. James observed this as they pulled in front of their destination. Only two of the six walled rooms had tin roofs. The rest were waiting for a change of fortune for the owner to finish the structure.

David stepped out to greet his honored guest. Children from around the quarter ran out of their yards crying, "Mundele," as they stared and pointed at James. He turned and responded to them with enthusiasm, which caused excited giggling and screaming.

"Good morning, Mr. James," he greeted. "This is my wife, Suzanne, and my sons."

James acknowledged the whole family and pulled out candy for the children from his belt pack, glad that he had included it with the rest of his supplies. He then stepped into the dark home, found a secluded corner, pulled out the burner, and made the call. Caleb answered on the second ring, and his voice came through clearer than James expected.

"Hey, bud. How are you managing over there? Congo must still be as crazy as ever if you're calling me for help."

"Crazier."

"Really? What's up?"

James proceeded to explain all that had happened in his first week. He shared about the two instances of the peeping Tom, the story about hearing the helicopter, and the main supervisor denying knowing anything about it. He spoke of Lucas' fears about the break in protocol and explained about the dead lesula. Finally, he expressed concern over Victor's warning about J.P. Walker.

Caleb absorbed all of it and asked several clarifying questions before getting to the most important one.

"So, what do you need me to do?"

"It's mainly investigative at this point," James replied. "Run a background check on Jim Pressman. I need to know who he really is. And, while you're at it, run one on J.P. Walker, too. I'd like to find out if the information I got about her can be corroborated. If so, I want details of who she's been involved with, whether or not those people are anyone we know or know of, and the beginning, middle, and end of those stories. Bottom line, I need you to warn me if you learn anything that suggests she could mess up my world." James took a breath before finishing with a plea, "Can you do this for me?"

"Sure, no problem. I'm going to need a secure way to contact you, though. Can we use encrypted text to keep in touch?"

"For now, I better reach out to you by phone. If you want to fall back on our code that we used two missions ago, I guess that could be a secure way to communicate through text or email. I believe only the two of us know that. Do you remember it?"

"Of course. I'm a bit rusty, but I actually have the key in an old journal. I'll pull it out today and send you a few practice messages. Listen, you know I think the world of you, and your family. Don't let your life be ruined over this."

"Copy that. You're the best, Caleb. Take care."

James clicked off the phone and walked out, shielding his eyes from the bright sunlight. He thanked David and said goodbye to his family. Hopping into the back seat of the Golf, he instructed Paul and Katey to take him home. The ride was nearly silent. Each man in the car knew the weight of the security and seriousness of this mission. No one was willing to break the quiet.

James stepped out at the gate, paid Paul in American dollars, and said goodbye. The rest of the day was spent in contemplation, mind mapping, and journaling. The process produced the realization that the following day would be his seventh since he arrived in Congo. *I haven't even been here a week yet.* James finished his thought with a deep sigh as he clenched and unclenched his fists several times. "This is going to be the longest mission ever," he quietly said out loud. "I just pray I come out unscathed."

Chapter 27

As soon as James' eyes popped open Sunday, right at 4:00 a.m., he remembered the Indian motorcycle that he had discovered in the shed. Once he was finished with his shower, he was determined to look up information on it. He was interested to see if the thing could be put back into good working order.

When his morning routine was complete, he plopped down in front of his laptop to look up the engine serial numbers that he had photographed. As he typed them in, a chart came up with every model and year in which that engine had been used. Scanning down the list, he finally found what he was looking for and was excited to see that the bike was a 1928 101-Scout. The description indicated that it was a forty-five inch, and he wondered if that was the tire size. He knew that with a bike that old, it would be difficult to find replacement parts, but James was willing to put in the extra time. He was hoping this could be both a hobby and a distraction from everything going on.

Looking up the history of the model, James found a site saying that it had been used for both military and traditional commercial purposes. This further excited him. He wondered if this particular bike had been part of the war effort that took place across Africa during the first and second World Wars. Clicking his computer shut, he thought he'd head over for his breakfast and gave himself assignments as he gathered his things. He would need to get permission from someone like Pressman to work on the bike. He also needed to figure out who it had belonged to and how it had been forgotten. The Indian led him back to thinking about the trap door in the depot, and he added that to his mental investigation list. He hoped to get over there again after breakfast to have a better look around. Maybe, he'd rope in Kongolo to watch the entrance for him while he tried to discover what was being concealed underneath.

James headed to the cafeteria knowing that hardly anyone would be up this early on a Sunday morning and that's when it hit him. Sundays were for worship, and he suddenly wondered if Lucas would want to do some sort of fellowship time with him.

Once inside, James found that he wasn't exactly alone. Victor was seated in his customary chair, and scooted up very close to him was J.P. Walker. When Victor caught James' glance, he looked down and moved his chair just an inch away from his early morning breakfast companion.

"Good morning, Victor. Hello, J.P.," James greeted. "How are you two doing? You're up early."

Victor gave James a tortured, beseeching look that almost begged for help. James knew in an instant that Victor wanted nothing to do with her. And when J.P. glanced up, the split-second glare of deep hatred aimed at him nearly took his breath away. He was not used to being treated like this by anyone.

A second later, the emotion was masked. Suddenly, she stood up and walked straight to James, close enough that he could feel her breath when she spoke. "Why don't you join us? We were just chatting about our best and worst relationships. I was telling Victor about the last guy I dumped. Come. Sit down."

"Sorry, ma'am," James said, "but I'm a creature of habit. Ask Victor. I always start my day tucked alone in that corner with my coffee and journal. How about I get a hint of that routine and maybe catch up with you later."

James got his drinks, fixed his bread, and headed to his usual spot, looking cool and confident but not feeling a bit of it. This woman disturbed him to the core. He couldn't point to a specific threat, but he had been trained to identify a dangerous enemy when he met one. There was something about J.P. Walker that radiated pure evil. Plus, Victor's warning added to his unrest. And exactly how she came to be on the compound and a part of the team was still a puzzle. He sat down, ready to be nourished both physically and spiritually, but could not focus. The last thing he wanted, though, was for his quiet time to be over and to join Victor and who he was already mentally calling the "she-devil."

He reread Psalm twenty-eight and Proverbs seven, knowing that he needed all the reinforcement he could get before walking back over to the table to rescue his new friend. He particularly honed-in on Psalm twenty-eight, verses three and seven: "Draw me not away with the wicked, and with the workers of iniquity, which speak peace to their neighbors, but mischief is in their hearts," and "The LORD is my strength and my shield; my heart trusted in Him, and I am helped." A good soldier understands enough about his own weaknesses to know when he needs reinforcement. Because he felt that J.P. was friendly with her words, but that evil plans were in her heart, he was also certain that God would be His most reliable personal protection from this woman.

With his journaling complete, and a prayer weighing heavy on his heart, James left his things on his table and took his coffee cup over to rescue his friend, all the while realizing he was putting himself in a precarious situation.

"God, help me!" he whispered under his breath.

Chapter 28

"Finish your breakfast yet?" James asked with a feigned ease as he sat down across from Victor and J.P.

"Ooh, come sit next to me," J.P. flirted. "Victor tells me you're a military man. I've always had a thing for soldiers, although I haven't seen you wearing a uniform. Why do you have to disappoint me, Jamesy?"

Clearly uncomfortable with the fact that she had given him a nickname, he chose to ignore both the undertones in her question and her request to move closer as he responded judiciously, "I'm U.S. military, but this is not a U.S. mission. I was instructed to leave my uniform behind. Just earth tones for me on this trip." James quickly followed up with a question obviously designed to take the attention off himself. "So, did you figure out which of you has a worse track record of broken hearts?"

"Definitely her," Victor accused, pointing at his seat companion. "She has a string of them, yet somehow manages to sound glib about her injured former sweethearts."

"Victor," J.P. shrilled, "for someone in similar circumstances as me, you sure are old-fashioned. Sweethearts indeed. They were simply men in my life for a season. That is all." She finished her sentiments rather callously.

"Victor does seem to have simple hopes in that area," James said, smiling. "We've managed to bring up relationships often in just one week of morning chats."

"So, who is your love interest, Jamesy?" J.P. asked. "A simple, all-American, girl-next-door?"

"Julia is far from simple," he responded a bit too defensively. "We've been friends since high school, and she's the only woman I've ever loved." He concluded with a quiet resolve.

"Love?" J.P. hissed. "Who falls in love in this day and age? Gosh, you're quaint, especially for a globe-trotting soldier. I take it you married this girl?"

"Yep. Six years ago. And we have two boys."

Victor jumped in. "I don't know, J.P. James seems pretty happy. Sounds like he's got a good thing going. We should all be that lucky."

James shot his friend an appreciative smile and a look that gave Victor courage to speak more freely. "Not everyone who comes from where we do feels that way. Some of us would rather have what you already do."

J.P. threw her head back and cackled at Victor's response. "You two sound like hopeless saps to me. Who thinks like that?"

The two answered simultaneously. "We do."

James continued. "The love I have for my family has given my life more purpose than I ever would have had without it."

"You guys are crazy," she said. "Let's get off the subject of love. I'm tired of it. What is your take on this mission? Do we really need to worry about these useless eaters succumbing to this disease?"

"Useless eaters? Never heard that term. Are you suggesting that the Congolese are not worth surviving the scourge?"

Victor piped up, addressing James' query. "'Useless eaters' is a term that has been bantered around for years by those who think that the planet is overpopulated. Several influencial leaders have suggested that we need to reduce the number to less than five hundred million in order to protect the globe from overuse. They fear that our world cannot support the current food and energy needs."

"You don't adhere to that philosophy, do you J.P?" James asked, shaking his head. "Certainly the Congolese are just as worthy of living as anyone."

"Don't tell me that you're going to judge me based on the fact that I share a well-accepted opinion," J.P. retorted.

"Hmm. Maybe I am," James admitted. "Life is precious. All life. The Congolese are just as valuable to God as you or me or Victor."

"What does God have to do with any of this? Are you a Bible-thumper, James? I did not expect a guy in your position to be so narrow minded."

"I'm a proud Bible-thumper, and there is no opinion that matters more to me than that of the Author of that book."

"I think you may be out of your league on this one, J.P.," Victor added.

She abruptly stood up with so much force that she knocked her chair over. "You two are a pair! Ganging up on me like that. I'm taking my breakfast back to the room. Victor, I'll talk to you later at the press meeting." J.P. grabbed her coffee and bread and stormed out the door, not bothering to pick up her chair. James and Victor looked at each other and said nothing until they were sure she was out of earshot. James started first with a quiet chuckle, but soon both were laughing until tears were falling, and they were nearly rolling on the floor.

When they regained their composure, Victor was the first to speak. "That was the most entertainment I've had since I've been here."

"Feeling's mutual," James replied. "I know you've already told me a little about her, but I'd like to know more. She's fascinating, but not necessarily in a good way. Can I text you later for a time to talk?"

"Sure. Whenever works for you."

"Great. I'll catch up later. Take care."

James fixed his second round of coffee and bread and returned to his table to wait for Lucas with a lot on his mind. J.P. Walker added an element to his security objectives that he had not previously considered. It was now clear that she had horrific views that could prove to turn into very malicious intentions.

Chapter 29

After his time with Lucas, James joined the small group of Samaritan's Purse team members for worship around ten o'clock in the lounge. Somehow, he managed to avoid even eye contact with J.P. for the rest of the day. His planned chat with Victor was scheduled for an hour before supper, and he was looking forward to learning more about this woman and her strange philosophies. Not knowing her well enough to actually believe that she was an enemy, he decided to study her perspective anyhow.

James succumbed to his afternoon habit of a short siesta. It usually took less than ten minutes to fall asleep, even with everything on his mind, and he figured twenty minutes was enough time to refresh himself from the heat and the worry. He spent the rest of the afternoon reviewing his notes, thinking about his new threat, and emailing Julia and Caleb.

At four o'clock he walked over to the cafeteria to down some water before his meeting with Victor who he ran into at the drink table. They chatted while preparing tea and bread. James teased Victor about observing high tea, and they both chuckled.

Once they were settled in a secluded corner of the lounge with their feet propped up on a coffee table, James started. "So, what do you think, Victor? Should I be worried about J.P. and her theories about the world population? Could she be here to act on them?"

"Well, her thoughts are not entirely original to her. If I remember correctly, the Nazis coined the term 'useless eaters,' or at least I think they've been credited with that gem. You might be surprised at how many in the intellectual community hold to the opinion that the world is overpopulated, and that some ethnic groups will need to be sacrificed for the good of the planet."

"Well, who decides who stays and who goes? I don't think anyone, short of God, deserves that kind of power. I mean, is that supposed to be a warped version of the survival of the fittest theory? And what's the criteria for who's fit and who's not? For the record, I'm kinda hoping that you don't know the answers to these questions."

Victor took a second to look at the floor before responding. When he glanced up, there was a strange expression in his eyes. "Actually, I believe that I do know who thinks that they are strong enough and smart enough to make such standards. But I'm very sure that I'm not supposed to be discussing this with an outsider. Will you let me defer answering that until I get to know you better?"

"Now you're freaking me out," James said.

"Sorry, mate. For now," Victor continued, "let me just drop a hint or two. Have you ever heard of the Georgia Guidestones? If I were you, I would start there. Study it. Study who put up the funding to build it. Many of the answers that you are seeking can be found there."

James scribbled a reminder in his notebook to look it up later. Now his curiosity was really piqued. "Is that all you're going to give me? Come on, man. Security of this mission is of utmost importance. If there are elements that could be working against the success of the response, I need to know everything."

"I'm sorry," Victor said. "That's the best I can do right now, but let me touch on J.P. for a minute. Like I said, be very careful around her. If you need me for anything concerning her, you can count on me. That's one thing I'm willing to help you on a hundred percent. I promise."

James accepted Victor's decline to answer, but he now had more questions than when he began. "Is this population concern only being addressed through disease or are there other factors that I need to know?"

"Well, another aspect is contraception. Some new techniques get tested first in third-world countries before being introduced in Western cultures. Maybe you should study a bit on that as well. But, honestly, you may be in over your head, here, James. Maybe you should just do the basics and not try delving into the deeper, bigger picture. Let things slide, for your own safety."

"Are you threatening me or warning me, Victor? I can't quite tell if you are being completely up front right now."

Victor leaned forward and said just above a whisper, "If any Westerner on this compound has your back, it's me. I'm not sure who else you can trust."

"How should I proceed?"

"If I were you, I would secure and strengthen my friendships with the Congolese and others not connected directly with this outbreak response. I understand that you hardly know me, but rest assured, I will tell you the truth, or at least a version of the truth that won't jeopardize myself." Looking steadily into James' eyes, Victor asked, "Do you understand what I am saying?"

James started to open his mouth, then quickly shut it again. He leaned back against the seat cushion and munched on his bread while studying Victor's face. He wanted to be positive this man was being forthcoming. Once he concluded that he was, he leaned forward again. "Ok. I will accept your answer and your assurance that you are on my side. I rarely trust someone so implicitly with such a short opportunity to get to know them, but it seems that I have little choice. Will you promise me something?"

"Depends on what you're asking."

"Can you at least give me specific warnings of any imminent dangers? I need all the help I can get."

"I can do that. I'm risking a lot here James, but for some reason, I like you and I want you to be able to get home to your wife and sons."

At this, James shuddered. He sucked in his breath and felt the muscles around his neck and shoulders tighten. There was that ugly thought again. The thought that finishing this mission would not be as straight-forward as he had been led to believe. He stood up, almost put his hand out to shake Victor's, then pulled it back again.

"You've given me more than I wanted to hear today, but I'm glad you decided to take a leap of faith and help me out. I appreciate it. Forgive me for cutting this short, but I'm going to go do some of that homework you suggested. Will I see you tomorrow at breakfast?"

"Sure, James. I understand. And yes, I'll be in my typical place in the morning. Take care."

Chapter 30

Another day dawned and James was up at four o'clock, preparing for his usual trek to the shower. He loved that first step out of his room in the dark of early morning with just a hint of lighter gray showing in the east. The air was cool and humid. He breathed in deeply, filled his lungs with oxygen, breathed out slowly until there was no breath left, and then he repeated the process. He did this three times. With each breath, he could detect different odors. First, was the pungent smell of a charcoal fire not far away. Next, he noticed the fragrance of a sweet flower. He wondered if it was the frangy-pangy which he got to know on his last trip to Congo. The final one was something being fried, and he instantly hoped they were having mikati for breakfast. James had learned to appreciate the locally-made donuts on that previous tour as well.

Stopping his breathing ritual and heading around the corner of the press building toward the shower area, he looked down for a split second to avoid tripping over a rock and, just as he had previously, nearly ran head on into J.P., who was once again wearing only a towel. Her hair was wet and hung around her neck. Before James had the chance to apologize, she allowed her towel to slip down a bit on the one side, nearly revealing more than he had ever hoped to see. She caught the towel and gave him a rather unreadable look.

"What are you trying to do, James? Get a glimpse of what lies beneath?"

James kept his eyes to the ground and continued walking. "Nope, just minding my own business," he responded with more embarrassment than he wanted to admit.

Just then, Kongolo stepped from around the corner, heading to work by the back pathway past the W.C. "Bonjour, James! How are you?"

"Good morning, Kongolo. Nice to see you." James breathed a sigh of relief. Having a familiar face appear added comfort just when he needed it.

J.P., not sure who this Kongolo was or how much he had seen, excused herself rather quickly. She rounded the corner of the press dorms leaving the two men watching her retreating, willowy figure.

"What was that?" Kongolo asked. "I saw her deliberately drop one side of her towel."

"Good," James uttered with a sigh of relief. "I'm glad to know I wasn't just imagining it. I saw the same thing. I'm thankful you came around the corner when you did. That woman scares me. Promise me that if you ever see her near me, that you come to my rescue." James tilted his head where she had been standing just a minute before.

"Of course. I am your man. You gave me my life back out there in Goma. I owe you everything. I promise to look out for you, sir."

"Thank you. Take care of yourself, Kongolo. We'll talk more later." James finished his morning routine and headed back to his room to prepare for the first part of his new day and week. To describe himself as disturbed would be an understatement. He cleared his throat several times to stop the choking dryness that suddenly overwhelmed him. James was determined to do more thinking and less physical activity. He was slipping into his "suspicion mode," becoming obsessed with learning more about his potential enemies, especially J.P. There were people he knew he could obviously trust and others he was certain that he could not. But everyone else he was just unsure of. He wondered how common the belief was that J.P. had and how many others might view Congolese as "useless eaters?" As he prepared for heading to the cafeteria, he seriously hoped he would not have any more close encounters with her.

James had several things on his agenda for the day, the first one being the weekly security team meeting that he had set up for each Monday at 9:00 a.m. in the lounge. Another item that he wanted to do was speak to Pressman about fixing up that Indian on his own time and money. At some point that week, he wanted to connect with the store owner, Amin, again. His last big priority was that dead lesula. He needed to study more about the disease itself and puzzle out why and how the monkey had contracted it. To think that testing was done on it and that it escaped, or worse, was released, was an idea that he did not really want to consider.

His early morning in the cafeteria was typical; quiet time with his coffee and a simple chat with Victor. It seemed that they both were eager to avoid the heavier topics of the weekend. James ate with Lucas who looked more somber than usual heading into the new week. At nine, James met with the Congolese and Uruguayan security team members. No new concerns were shared. Updates were reported on the cutting back of trees and the addition of the razor wire.

While a bit confused and somewhat reluctant, Pressman ultimately agreed to let James fix up the Indian motorcycle. With the leeway granted, James decided to use an hour after lunch to pull out the bike and extra motor, clean it up, and haul it over to his room. He certainly had plenty of space for the repair job, and the urge to work in front of a fan was strong.

Immediately after lunch, he reiterated to Kongolo the importance of keeping an eye out for any time he noticed that J.P. was nearby. James then headed to the depot. While he still intended to investigate the tunnel below the trap door, today was all about the bike. He wanted to decipher a way to maneuver it out of the spot it was wedged into near the back of the small structure. There was so much junk between it and the door that he knew extracting it would be no easy feat. Like before, he opened the front door, again admired its well-oiled hinges, and walked to the back to prop open the window. Light and air flooded the heavy atmosphere inside the room. James breathed deeply, hoping that nothing more toxic than diesel fumes lingered there.

He made his way back to the motorcycle and studied the area around it and the pathway between it and the door. First, he removed the items leaning on or near the bike and then pulled out the floor rag that he borrowed from the kitchen staff and wiped off the initial cobwebs, checking carefully to make sure they were uninhabited. Getting bit by a spider or scorpion was not on his to do list. He then wiggled the bike forward out of its wedged position. Once on the tiny pathway between the junk, James was able to carefully push it toward the door. Outside, he took a moment to wipe his brow before heading back in to haul out the spare motor. Having already determined the year and model from the engine numbers, he got introspective when he thought for a minute about the history that this machine had witnessed throughout the last nearly nine decades, and wished the thing could talk and share its story.

Now equipped with all the parts, James was able to do a proper initial assessment of the bike's condition. The most obvious need was that of new tires. They were so dry rotted that they were nearly flaking apart. He knew that ordering new tires would be top priority. Realizing he needed tools, he decided to walk back in to see if he could locate wrenches or a socket set and some pliers. He was able to find everything he needed with little difficulty since there was an ancient tool bag near where the bike had been resting.

By the door, he found some bottles of used motor oil, probably saved for general lubrication tasks. He grabbed one of these out, too, and pushed the motorcycle to his room by the far end of the cafeteria building to avoid as many eyes as possible. The urge to keep his project a secret seemed important to him, although he didn't really know why.

Struggling to move it over the rough grass as he rounded the corner between the main building and press dorms, James took a second to look over the courtyard to assess who was in sight. No one was crossing the area that he could see. He deftly pushed the bike across the clearing, unlocked his door, and got the bike inside. Once deposited there, he went back for the engine and supplies and closed up the depot.

Tucked back in his room, he pulled off his soaked shirt, turned the fan directly on himself, and sat in a chair in front of the machine with a notebook and pencil. He took an hour carefully studying over the Indian, taking notes, and making a more detailed assessment of the repair needs. He wondered if any motorcycle mechanics lived in the village. An hour before supper, he cleaned himself up a bit and sat in the wicker chair with his feet elevated, doing some deeper overall thinking about everything that had happened in his first week.

James looked through every journal entry, took time to review his encrypted notes, and perused the emails he had sent and received. Relistening to the recording he made of his conversation with Caleb, he realized he had some serious subjects to evaluate and some mental detective work to do. Unfortunately, that required him to do something he had promised himself he never would, so James added poking around the dark web to his list. There were some items he felt he could just get more straight-forward answers to outside of traditional internet access.

When he was all thought out, he headed over for supper, looking forward to spending time with his new friend, Lucas. He wanted to delve into his more-than-usual somber attitude. James let out another irritated sigh as he locked his door behind him and headed across the courtyard. He sure hoped he wouldn't still be in Congo when those mangoes ripened. With that thought, he felt his stomach drop and his heart begin a heavy, dull pounding.

Chapter 31

"Hey Lucas," James greeted as he placed his drinks down at his corner spot. "How are things today at the clinic? Any better? Making progress?"

"Not so good, I would say," Lucas responded with a quieter, more subdued voice. "Go get your supper, and we can talk before the others join us."

James picked up his plate from the counter that was already filled with food, then grabbed a second, smaller plate and loaded it with bread. He headed back to his table with a heavy heart, knowing that the situation would only get more complicated with Lucas' update.

"So, what's on your mind?"

"Couple of things," Lucas responded. "One is that we don't seem to be making headway at the clinic. The sick patients are not recovering, even with the vaccine, and more people are becoming ill each day. My other concern is that dead lesula. I've been thinking a lot about the fact that it was infected and what it was doing inside the compound walls."

"Let's tackle that first subject: the not improving patients," James began. "Why do you think this is happening? Is the vaccine not powerful enough to stop the progression of the fever? And how does the disease keep popping up in the village? You know more about the science behind these issues than I do."

Lucas stopped mid-bite and stared at James. "Why did you suggest that the vaccine was not powerful enough? It was tested extensively in the west African outbreak and was proven effective toward ending that crisis."

"I think it's a fair question," James defended, a little taken aback at his friend's unexpected response. "I don't know. Maybe things are not as they appear. What if the vaccine is not up to the approved strength? And what if that lesula was used for testing and was released intentionally?"

"What you're saying is diabolical," Lucas pushed back. "That would be the worst act of sabotage in human history. I can be pretty cynical, but that's a little too extreme. Even by my standards."

James nodded and opened his mouth to interject, but Lucas was on a roll.

"I can't imagine anyone powerful enough to pull off an experiment like that because it involves too many people. However, if what you're saying is true, I'm getting on the next plane out of here. My life and that of my family are too important to me."

"Slow down," James implored. "I can't have you bailing on me. I need you to help me get to the bottom of things. You're my eyes and ears on the inside of the clinic. Come on now."

Lucas dropped his gaze and simply said, "Sorry."

James coaxed, "I understand you're worried, but you know that this virus could easily spread around the globe. Just because you're safe in Miami with your family does not mean that you're completely free from danger. You need to stick with me on this."

"I understand," Lucas conceded.

"If I'm worried about your safety at any point," James said, "I'll tell you to take off. I'm like you, bro! I got a lot riding on my success here. We need to look at the bigger picture, which ultimately includes our families."

Lucas sighed and dropped his head. "You're right. I'm sorry. It's just that I've never been this frightened before. I'm not a soldier like you. I have little experience with real enemies. Listen, here come our colleagues. Let's pick this up another time. And promise me you'll tell me when to jump ship."

"I will."

James and Lucas resorted to small talk as their friends gathered around, but they knew their conversation wasn't over.

After supper, James locked himself in his room for the night. He emailed Julia, texted pictures of the compound to the boys, and spent the rest of his time surfing the internet for tips on parts and repair for the motorcycle. He just needed to give his brain a break and focus on something smaller. Tomorrow was another day to worry about this continually thickening plot.

Chapter 32

The rest of that second week flew by with James' clear vision for the security of the mission and with the repairing of the motorcycle to distract him. He found the spark plug he needed on Amazon as well as new tires to replace the originals. He sent links for both to Julia and asked her to please order them and have them sent to Sebastian in Kinshasa. He then emailed his friend, letting him know those items would be coming, so someone would need to be on the lookout for their arrival. After he had cleaned up both the engine and the spare, he planned the tasks to be completed over the following week.

On Wednesday morning, James had another in-depth discussion with Victor about the value of human life and the disturbing depopulation theories. Victor cited some speeches by famous world leaders who considered the lowering of the global population a good thing. James was still baffled at the idea that some people thought that they reserved the right to make such decisions on behalf of everyone else. He couldn't fully grasp the concept that some really believed that their lives were more valuable than the lives of others. When he asked how Victor thought those leaders would initiate such a plan, he simply said that the right major crisis would bring the world to a place where the general population would actually welcome the control that would be provided by them and allow them to do whatever they wanted. While James wrapped his mind around that thought, he planned another trip to the village to chat with Amin and make another phone call to Caleb. He figured he'd combine both tasks the same morning.

Friday dawned overcast from the dry season's typical cooler weather. James loved it, but his Congolese friends looked like they were close to freezing into a solid state. Katey and Paul met him at the front gate in heavy windbreakers. Both were shivering when James climbed into the back seat of the Golf.

"Mbote na bino!" James greeted. "How are you two? You look like popsicles."

"Monsieur," Katey confessed, "we in Congo are not accustomed to this temperature. We are very cold, both my brother and me."

James chuckled and shook his head affectionately at his foreign buddies before changing gears. "Let's go see Amin," James directed. "I want to discuss with you three the tensions in the village. Peace is a vital part of my security mission, you know."

"Yes. We are already headed to Amin's. He always drinks coffee on the store veranda at this time of the morning. I am hoping, he will invite us to join him," Katey said, looking forward to the possibility of a warm drink.

As they were pulling up to the brightly-colored building in the small commercial district of Domiongo, James noticed that Paul was correct. Amin was sitting out front with his son, drinking coffee, and looking at his cell phone. He raised his head when the car pulled up.

"Welcome, my new friend." Amin gestured with one hand for him to have a seat. He sent his son back to the kitchen to tell his mother that guests were here, and that more coffee would be needed.

Katey and James sat down in the two chairs that were available. Paul pretended to be minding his own business by playing a game on his phone while still seated in the car.

"How are you, James?" Amin asked. "How is your job working out?."

"Things are okay," James said. "I'd like to get some questions answered, though, which is why we're here. First and foremost, what's your take on the villagers?"

The blank stare and silence James received caused him to clarify.

"What I mean is, do you feel like they are worried about the mission? Have you heard of any new concerns?"

"Nothing specific I'm aware of, but I do notice a continued frenzy in the tone of the conversation regarding everything related to it.

People are very anxious. Those with sick family members at the clinic are saying that their loved ones are not being properly cared for."

"Okay."

Amin went on, "I am very worried. If their fears are not addressed, I am afraid that they will do something drastic."

"Like what?" James asked, leaning closer and lowering his voice.

"I have heard from my house boy that the village is thinking of confronting the officials at the compound concerning the treatment of their families."

"I see."

"The village chief is being coerced into bringing charges against the mission. He has been in contact with a well-known lawyer in Kinshasa."

"Hmm. That's a problem," James said. "Have you heard anything about this, Katey?"

"Yes, last night when I was walking home late from the market after dark. I could not see the face of the speaker, though. What Amin says is very true. The village seems to be nearly ready to take things into their own hands."

James then turned back to Amin, "Can I ask you to keep me informed? I need to know of any specific plans you may become aware of."

Amin heartily agreed. "Of course. Remember, your success is

vital to the health of my family and the prosperity of my business. Without you, our whole village is in danger, maybe the whole region."

The two of them exchanged emails and confirmed cell numbers. The highly anticipated coffee arrived along with some fresh mikati donuts. Everyone enjoyed the refreshments and some casual conversation as customers began to approach the store. The rest of the chat steered toward simple things: family, sports, and international news. They even touched on the World Cup qualifiers. James was more in tune with soccer news than most Americans.

The men finished their drinks and said goodbye.

They headed across town to David's house to make the phone call to Caleb. James updated him on the past week and his new concerns about possible sabotage. Caleb listened, took copious notes, and promised to research things as much as possible on his end. The call ended with their typical sentiments of brotherhood and support. James turned back to the car, rejuvenated by his morning off the compound and sad to be returning to the oppressive weight of his task. He sighed as he plopped into the back seat of the Golf, heaviness settling on him like a dense mantle.

Chapter 33

By the time Sunday rolled around, James couldn't believe that it had only been two weeks since he last saw Julia and the boys. A sinking feeling deep in his stomach plagued him when he thought of them; a nameless dread that created an unexplained sweat and an unusually quick need to swallow often; almost like the emotion was choking the life out of him.

As James remembered, most people on the compound were sleeping in because it was the weekend, so he found himself eating breakfast alone. At nine, the Christian group gathered in the lounge for a time of worship. James had rather easily talked Victor into joining them. They sang songs together through the help of YouTube videos, and Lucas brought a devotional on God being man's defense from Psalm 94:22. Victor seemed to enjoy the hearty singing and listened quietly to the expounding of the psalm.

After lunch, James took his typical siesta, but he kept it short, craving time to work on the bike. The parts were supposed to arrive early that week on a flight from Kinshasa, and he wanted everything as ready as possible for the repairs. After supper, as the sun was just starting to dip down in the western sky, James got a text from Amin as he was sitting outside his door.

> My friend, I am texting to warn you that the villagers are extremely angry. My employee has heard that they plan to force their way into the compound tonight to remove their sick family members. Be warned!

"Oh, dear God, help us." James expressed out loud, just as Victor was walking past.

"What the heck, James?" Victor exclaimed. "I've never heard you sound that exasperated. What's going on?"

James pulled him close and handed him his phone. Victor's response was a low whistle and a few more-expressive words. "Well, we can't let that happen. It could make a bad situation turn worse in only a few hours What are you going to do?"

James held up a finger while he took his phone back from Victor and called Katey. As soon as he heard his friend pick up, James started in before he could even speak. "What have you heard about a mob planning to storm the compound this evening?"

"I am on my way in Paul's car with a few of my soldiers," Katey responded. "I am only minutes ahead of the group. They are very hostile. Assemble the U.N. soldiers near the gate and meet me there as soon as you can!"

Victor heard every word and sprang into action as soon as James hung up. "I'll notify Facundo. Should the rest of the mission be aware of what's going on?"

"No. But advise Pressman. And meet me at the gate the second you are able."

Victor headed off to gather Facundo and his unit and warn Pressman. James strapped on his knife and hid it under his belt. He headed down the path while texting a thank you to Amin for his warning and arrived at the gate just as Katey was stepping out of the Volkswagon. Paul, deciding that it was too dangerous to go back to town through the mob, drove north along the wall and parked far enough away to be safe but close enough to get a good view of the front gate. Soon Facundo, his men, and Pressman joined them along with Victor.

"What should we do, James?" Facundo asked.

"Yes, do you want me to speak to the mob?" Pressman inquired.

"No, I need you to stay near and help Facundo and his group on the inside of the gate," James ordered. "Facundo, be prepared to use any peaceful but forceful means necessary to keep this group outside of the compound. If they succeed, not only will the village be threatened, but our lives as well. Victor and Katey, are you two ready to step out of the gate with me to handle this situation?"

Both men nodded. James instructed Katey to speak to the crowd and translate their concerns since his Lingala was limited.

Katey agreed. They could hear the group coming down the path toward them. Their loud voices were violent. The three stepped outside the gate to await the dangerous enemy. Facundo, his men, and Pressman looked white with fear.

"Lock the gate. Keep them out no matter what!" James instructed, forced to shout over the crowd noise.

Victor stared at James incredulously. "You're making us very vulnerable by having us stand on the outside of a locked gate," he yelled back, surpassing James' volume. "You are crazy, man."

James gave him a searching look, then turned to face the approaching crowd.

Chapter 34

Katey spoke first. He addressed the village chief who stood near the front of the mob. "Chief Jean! Mbote na yo! Why are you here, sir?"

"You know why I am here," the man responded in a language that James did not recognize. "We are here to remove our sick family members from the clinic. You know that they are not being treated with proper respect and medical care."

Katey took a second to translate this to James and Victor, loud enough for the men inside the gate to hear his words. Katey asked in the dialect, "What exactly are your concerns? In what way are your families not being treated right?"

The man gave an anger-infused answer that caused the crowd to cheer with vehemence and shake their weapons, mostly machetes. Victor stood silently, taking in the scene. He had never been this terrified in his whole life, and he had covered some pretty harrowing global events. He knew the intensity of an African mob and really feared for his life. One glance at James, though, gave him a spark of confidence. He stood tall and appeared to be completely calm. Victor also noticed the knife tucked under his belt. Somehow knowing that James was armed gave him courage as well.

Katey translated the chief's response. "The men say that they have heard that on several occasions, the doctor did not properly sterilize between patients. They feel that they could take better care of their sick family members at home. They insist on our letting them in to take them away."

James spoke with authority, directing his words to the leader of the village, and Katey continued to translate both sides of the conversation. "Chief Jean, please know that your accusations are being investigated. We will find who is responsible for the breach in protocol. We will prosecute them according to the law. I promise you this."

"We want justice now!" an angry young man shouted from the back of the mob. "Let us take our families, or we will kill you and break down the gate. Get out of the way, mundele!"

The crowd erupted, but the chief silenced them with a strong rebuke. He would not tolerate a teenager speaking for him and the village leadership. Turning to James, he continued, "How can you guarantee that you will bring us justice and keep our family members safe? And will you make yourself accountable to me?"

Through Katey, James reiterated his promise and said that he would personally inspect the clinic and search for answers to their concerns. He vowed to keep in phone contact with the chief and communicate all the results. The chief seemed placated, but the rest of the crowd was eager for action. The voice rose again from the back. "You cannot make friends with this enemy, Chief! We want results tonight. American soldier, you must let us past, or you will all be sorry!"

As the chief turned to rebuke the young man again, another impulsive teen let a broken brick fly. The piece hit Victor directly in the temple, causing his knees to buckle and nearly making him collapse. Katey caught him under the arm and held him up.

James reacted instantly. He walked straight through the crowd to the assailant. "You're coming with me." James grabbed the young man's arm with a vise-like grip and forcefully yanked him to the front. His commanding presence and obvious physical strength temporarily quieted the mostly youthful mob. The group made a path for James and the struggling member who was being humiliated in front of the villagers.

"Look what you have done," James exclaimed, reverting to simple Lingala. He forced the young man to look at Victor's profusely bleeding head. "Your actions have injured an innocent man."

With this, the chief decided to add his opinion to the situation by smacking the youth so hard that he went flying onto his back. The rest of the crowd took a step away from the scene as they witnessed this sudden change in the mood of their leader.

He turned and addressed the rioters. "I am chief in this village. I say what does and does not happen. There will be no more violence unless I order it. Is that clear?"

Every member of the mob silently and numbly agreed. They knew their chief, and they understood that this smack would not be the young man's only punishment for what he had done. And though they feared for their friend, they feared more for themselves. When the chief told them to return to the village, they did so without argument. He then turned to James. "Do you promise to call me in the morning to report how the injured man is doing? Here is my cell phone number." The chief handed James a business card with his contact information on it.

James agreed . The chief and his deputy left, dragging the condemned attacker, who took with him his wounded pride, back to the village. James, Victor, and Katey pounded on the locked gate, stepped inside with Paul who had pulled his car forward, and leaned hard against the brick wall of the compound. They clearly had much to discuss.

Chapter 35

"First, Victor, let's have a look at that wound," James said, still controlling the situation with precision. "Katey, can you point that over here?" Katey shined the flashlight on Victor's head, and the whole group gathered around to inspect the injury. Paul, Facundo, Pressman, and the others leaned in for a better look.

"I'd like to keep the seriousness of this event tonight as quiet as possible," Pressman stated, his face somber and melancholy as he spoke. "It needs to be limited to this group, and maybe whichever doctor stiches Victor up."

"Why do you think it should be kept a secret?" James asked while dabbing Victor's still-bleeding wound, dipping his handkerchief repeatedly in bottled water. "Are you afraid that it will spook the rest of the response team?"

"Exactly." Pressman responded. "They're here to do a job. Being distracted by a risk to their own security won't help them do their assignments any better."

James acquiesced while Pressman made clear to the U.N. team that they were not to speak of the incident to the other members of the mission. James didn't like it at all. But he was keeping his own secrets, and he was certain that the villagers would continue to talk about the night's event for weeks to come. He was sure some of it would trickle back to the compound.

"Come on, Victor; let's get you to my room where we'll have some privacy. I'll get Lucas to come examine you. I think that the bleeding has almost stopped."

Victor nodded his agreement.

James continued, "Can you walk without any help? I guess even a stagger might raise suspicions from others."

Victor spoke for the first time since the injury. "I'm fine. I got this."

He and James said goodbye to Katey and Paul for the night as Pressman walked ahead toward the main buildings. Facundo and his men set a watch near the front gate in case any angry stragglers were lurking about.

Once James had Victor seated on his wicker chair with a bottle of water, he went to fetch Lucas. A knock on his room door brought Pierre first, his Congolese roommate. Lucas was asked to follow James on the guise of showing him the work he had done so far on the motorcycle. Once they were securely in James' room, the truth was fully explained.

Lucas' forehead wrinkled as he furrowed his eyebrows listening to James. Without a word, he began examining Victor's wound. "This looks deep. I should probably do a few stitches. What kind of stuff do you have in that medical kit, James? Sutures? Some type of topical anesthetic?"

"Both."

"We can't afford to have Victor yelping if we're trying to keep things secret," he added with a smirk.

"You make me sound like a baby," Victor protested. "But a bit of something to numb it would be appreciated. Wait, do you have any of that glue stuff? It would leave less of a scar that way."

"Do you mean New-Skin?" James asked. "If so, I don't."

Lucas turned to James. "Do you know where any super glue is? That's basically the same thing."

"Easy," James answered walking over to his long worktable where things were assembled for repairing the bike. He handed Lucas the small tube and asked how he could help.

"I've cleaned it up. Could you hold it together? I'll keep patting it dry as I apply the glue. Victor, your job is to sit super still." With the three of them working together, Victor was soon mended. They continued to sit there, discussing the near riot on the compound.

"Way to stay calm out there, man. Impressive."

"Years of practice, Victor," James replied, before admitting, "Truth is, the confidence was a mask for how worried I actually was."

"I'm sure that poor lad you dragged out of the crowd is severely regretting his decision about now."

"I hear you," James said. "Probably getting a sound beating."

"Yep,"

"Can't help feeling a bit sorry for the kid. I'm sure he didn't plan on it ending up the way it did."

"So, tell me," Lucas said, "the whole thing from the beginning. How did you know this was going to happen? Why were you even outside the gate?"

James told him about Amin's warning and said that Victor happened to be standing there when the tip was given. He had put things into action quickly by mobilizing Facundo and his men and notifying Pressman. Katey had arrived with his brother only a few minutes ahead of the incensed mob.

"I had Victor, Katey, and myself outside the gate," James explained. "Facundo's group just inside ready to use whatever means necessary to prevent the rioters from invading the compound. I needed Katey to help translate, and I figured that as a reporter, Victor would want a front row to the action. I just didn't think that he would get injured. Sorry, bro."

"No need to apologize. I'm glad I was there, but with the gag order that Pressman placed us under, I can hardly report on it. Still, I might type something up and be ready to push 'send' if things take a downward spiral. The media is not used to being hushed so unceremoniously."

"Yeah, that's tough," Lucas said. "I could ask why he would require secrecy, but aren't we doing the same thing with that monkey? Something like that can't be hidden for long, however. Even if you guys say nothing, the kitchen and compound workers from the village will be hearing about it from their families when they're off duty. It can't really be kept from the international staff."

"You're right there," Victor affirmed. "Well, gentlemen, I think I need to retire for the evening. I'm going to fill up my water bottles and grab a cup of tea. I'll make up some story about hitting my head on my desk if someone asks about the bandage. Good night."

After he left, James and Lucas spent a few minutes reflecting on the evening. They spoke again about the dead lesula and how it came to be where they had found it. Lucas still had not learned anything by just keeping his ears open.

James made an appointment for eleven o'clock the next morning to do a tour of the clinic and medical offices. Both agreed that he would need to take a more aggressive approach to finding solutions. Once Lucas left, James spent the next hour sipping water, calming his nerves, and writing a thorough report of the evening's events. He sent a brief email to Fitzpatrick informing him about the riot attempt. Pressman had told them to keep the events a secret, but James took that to mean only from the people on the compound, so he didn't feel like he was breaking any rules. Besides, he wasn't sure who he could trust here, but he knew who had his back on the other side of the globe.

Chapter 36

"Another day in Congo," James said to himself as soon as his eyes popped open at ten minutes 'til four. His third Monday since arriving. He laid in bed for just a moment to wake his brain and think through the events of the previous evening. It had taken him a while to unwind, and when he had finally fallen asleep, it was disturbed by the thought of that poor boy receiving a sound beating. Bothered to think that he endured more pain than just the humiliation of being pulled to the front of the mob by an American soldier, James sighed and allowed his shoulders to slump for a minute, rubbing his hands over his face as he rolled out of bed.

Once his feet were in flipflops, he turned on the small corner lamp and glanced around the room. A deep desire to not want to face the challenges on the other side of the door sunk over him like a heavy flak jacket. Knowing that he needed to keep his word to the village chief and investigate the incidents of broken protocols at the clinic, he shuddered to think of being so close to that deadly virus.

After his shower, he headed to the cafeteria to plan and prepare for his day. His first agenda was his weekly security forces meeting at nine. Then, he needed to obtain permission to investigate the events that Lucas had shared. He was not sure how to get it without revealing too much of Lucas' privacy and security, all of which he pondered as he stepped into the lit room that was becoming a welcoming friend. Coffee, bread, and growing relationships were transforming this cafeteria into a haven.

James was surprised to see Victor there so early. "Good morning. I can't believe you're here in spite of what you've just been through. Or is that why you're up?"

"Yeah, I had trouble sleeping," Victor admitted. "And when I woke up, it felt like a massive weight was sitting on my skull. I'm wondering if I have a slight concussion."

"You might."

Victor went on. "I'm going to take it easy for a day or so. Rest. Give myself time to heal. How are you?"

"Okay, I guess. Took me a while to let everything go last night, too. I still can't help but feel concerned about what probably happened to that kid. Congolese beatings are not easy to endure. I know that from personal experience."

"You were beaten in Congo? I didn't hear that story. Was it when you were here on your last mission?"

"Yup. It happened that first night Julia and I were in the rebel encampment. Six years ago. But I still easily remember how terrified I was."

"I'll let you get your breakfast, James. But sometime, I'd like to hear that whole story about your abduction."

"You've got it."

The two men went about their morning routines quietly until the rest began to trickle in. James ate breakfast with the American team members. He decided that he was not going to ask Pressman's permission to investigate Lucas' issues. After all, his mandate was the security of the mission and that should be all he needed to move forward. In this case, it would be easier to ask for forgiveness rather than permission, anyway.

At nine, he met with the U.N. security unit. They had many questions for James, Facundo, and Katey about the mob the evening before. It was clear that the team's morale was deeply disturbed by the reality of the compound being physically threatened by the villagers. James assured them that he would investigate the chief's concerns and would work to develop a good relationship with the village leadership. Once the group was placated, they noticeably relaxed. James tasked them with keeping their ears to the ground about any further threats and to report directly to Facundo and himself if they heard anything.

After the meeting, James had an appointment with Lucas at the medical offices near the front gate of the compound. His investigation would begin with a tour and questioning the staff. A Congolese guard was out front, someone James did not recognize. "Mbote! Ozali malamu?"

"Ehh, nazali malamu, monsieur. But I do know English. I wish to practice," the man said.

"What's your name? I don't think we've met before."

"I am Petit Jean. This is my first day as sentinel. I was only transferred to the Domiongo unit just last week from Kinshasa. Truly, sir, I am nervous about this assignment."

"I'm glad to meet you, Petit Jean," James said. "Yes, I understand your concern about being so close to the virus. Have you been told about the safety protocol?"

"Yes, sir. I was informed of this today when I arrived."

"Good," James affirmed. "I'm heading inside the office building to meet my friend for a tour of the operation. Stay safe."

The soldier nodded as he walked through the front door. Lucas was just inside as he had promised he would be. James sighed imperceptibly as he stepped forward to meet him, ready to get this part of the process over with.

Chapter 37

"Hey Lucas. Hope today's tour sheds some light on the things that are bothering not only you, but also the villagers."

"Me too, James. Me too. Let's start with the offices. I really don't think that you should enter the clinic, but I have arranged for you to speak to the staff that are working there."

"Sounds good."

"They'll come over here to talk with you individually," Lucas continued. "I also took the time to sketch a layout of the rooms in the clinic, so you can have a visual idea of what it's like in there."

"Show me that diagram first. Do you have an office somewhere?"

"The English-speaking medical staff share one just through here. That's where we'll start the tour, then we'll go through the other offices, and finally end up at the testing lab which has a back-door entry, making it easy to transfer specimens from the clinic to that room. They are really taking steps to curb the spread of the virus, except, of course, with the events that I have shared with you. Here's that diagram. I actually have it with me."

James took the paper from Lucas and greeted several of the staff scattered around the room at different workstations as they made their way through the facility. He noticed that each had their own laptop, which was being put to good use. James acknowledged the people he knew and was introduced to several others. Lucas showed him the location on the diagram of the clinic building where he had exited and did not find the person waiting to rinse him down.

"Is it the same staff member every time?" James inquired. "Did you ask anyone about it?"

Lucas led him back out into the hallway for privacy before answering. "I haven't shared this breach in protocol with my colleagues. Actually, no. It is not the same person each time. That's why I haven't been able to figure out the source of the problem."

"So maybe a proper safety precaution would be to assign one person to that task, but that goes on the list for later. Let's focus on discovering who dropped the ball. Is it always a Congolese who performs the sanitizing procedure?"

"Yes," Lucas confirmed, "a health worker trained by the government and assigned this job."

"Well then, let's see if we can find a personnel list for those employees. With their names and a duty log, we can call them out one at a time and hit them with a series of similar questions and see if any anomalies or leads surface. But maybe we shouldn't let them speak to each other. I don't want them getting a chance to line their stories up."

Lucas led James out to the shade of a large mango tree about twenty yards away from the clinic after retrieving the personnel file and work log. He asked James to wait a minute while he found the first person on the list. He went back inside and then emerged with a Congolese man who appeared to be in his twenties. James checked his name on the personnel log and asked him about the dates that Lucas had mentioned. The man said that he had gotten sick with malaria and was not even on the compound during those times.

The next worker was a mother in her forties with four children in school. She too had an excuse for the dates in question.

The third employee, however, produced the anomaly James was waiting for. The young man's name was Christophe. He was twenty-five and new to the village of Domiongo, having only moved there as part of the crisis response. When asked why he was not in place to sanitize Lucas, the man appeared worried. He looked at the ground and mumbled something.

"What did you say? Olobi nini?" James asked.

"I was at the back door at the time. I had permission. I promise!"

"Permission to do what?" James almost barked.

"I was at the back door of the clinic to meet a buyer. I was given permission to sell some medicines that were nearly expired. I was told that I could do this to earn a little extra money and that no one would notice. That day was the first time it happened."

"Who gave you permission?" James demanded. "What was the person's name?"

"I don't know," Christophe defended. "I see him here very rarely. That day, I had a friend from the village come. A note was given to me that he was waiting by the back door while Dr. Jackson was in with patients. Although I knew that I was not to leave the sanitation post, the message was insistent. I left only long enough to gather the medicines that I had already put aside. The friend paid me American dollars then went back to the village to sell to a pharmacy. I was only gone ten minutes."

"Can you describe him?" James pushed further.

"He is a mundele, but he is not from America or Britain. I did not recognize his accent even though he spoke English. He is rather tall. About as tall as you."

"Is there anything about his face that you remember? The color of his eyes or hair or any unusual features?"

"His hair is lighter than yours," Christophe answered. "And I do remember that he had… I don't know how to say it in English… but he had a line here." The Congolese man paused while he took his finger and made a vertical line in the middle of his chin and lower lip. "I'm not sure what you call that in English."

Lucas looked at James. "Is he saying the guy has a cleft in his chin?"

"Yes." James Immediately connected the dots.

"Christophe, were you on duty each of these dates after that as well?"

Ashamed, he quietly nodded his head, affirming that he was.

Lucas suddenly became concerned. "Are you going to fire him? He thought that he was doing something permissible."

"I believe that he should be replaced," James said. "His indiscretion put you and patients at risk. Hardly someone to trust with that responsibility going forward." He turned to Christophe, "I'm sorry. You need to be removed from your post. Still, I hate to see you lose your job."

"Please, monsieur! I need this employment. I have a wife and young child in Kinshasa depending on my income. I am sorry if I did something wrong."

"You did do something wrong," James stated matter-of-factly. "I have an idea though. If I continue to let you work here, it must be under two conditions."

"Whatever you say, sir."

"I need you to tell your friend in the village that you can no longer sell him medicine. Also, I need you to work for me. Can you report to whenever you see this man again that told you to do this? I will give you my cell number. If you see anything suspicious going on near the clinic, I need you to tell me. Can you do that?"

"Yes. Anything." Christophe promised. "Thank you, sir, for giving me a second chance. I will not let you down."

Christophe and James exchanged numbers. James sent him back to work while Lucas and he chatted.

"Do you know who he's talking about?"

"Not by name," James said, "but I'm pretty sure I've seen his face. I woke up and caught someone peeking in my bedroom window twice. The second time was just a few days ago. I managed to get a glimpse of him before he turned away, and his chin definitely had a cleft in it. When I chased him, I lost him in the woods behind the press dorm. Christophe is the only solid connection that I have to this mysterious person since, to my knowledge, he is not a member of the response team. I know I backtracked a little on the whole employment thing, but he genuinely seemed sorry."

"Yeah, I agree with you. Like I said, I didn't want to see him lose his job either."

After deciding to discuss everything further at a later date and time, the two men parted ways. James headed back to his room to report his latest findings. Lucas returned to his office and research. They both knew this was only one small piece in a very large and complex puzzle.

Chapter 38

James stepped into his room, looked carefully around, then closed the door. For the first time since he had arrived, it occurred to him to scan his room for bugs, and not the creepy-crawly kind. He wondered if his being here was a blockade to the plans of a more sinister enemy than Ebola. His quick gaze sought the likeliest places to plant a listening device or camera.

First, he checked all the outlets, vents, and objects that were in the room before his arrival, then he carefully scrutinized the knots in the wood of his clothes cabinet, and examined the mechanisms of the ceiling light, as well as the plumbing of his small sink. Lastly, he checked the wicker chair and footstool, turning the pieces upside down and inspecting everything diligently. Nothing.

He stopped to consider the types of surveillance devices that could possibly be used. As a communications expert in the Special Forces, it was his job to keep up on the latest advances in technology. *It wouldn't have to be a camera,* he thought to himself. *What I'm doing inside this room is of little importance. It could be something monitoring my internet communications or a listening device. Those would be harder to detect. In fact, the audio surveillance could even be done from outside if it was close enough to the room to pick up my conversations.*

With that, James went to scan the small patch of forest surrounding the back part of his chamber. That was the area of the boot print he had seen earlier, so it seemed like a good place to start.

It only took five minutes to locate the laser microphone. *This guy was pretty sloppy,* James thought. Plucking the device from the underside of a branch of the closest mango tree, he took it inside. The microphone had been attached in such a way as to have the laser beam pointed directly at the wall above where his laptop sat. He made a mental note to check his hard drive for any type of weird, embedded software, knowing that they often were installed through a virus or malware. It was also close enough to have picked up anything he had said out loud. He stopped to think back to any conversations that would have tipped people off as to the specifics of what he was investigating. Realizing that the most interesting ones would have been those he had made to Caleb, which he had done on the other side of the village, that precaution was certainly wise in hindsight.

With the magnifying glass app on his phone, he studied the device, looking for a serial number and knowing that this type of microphone employed interferometry, a technique in which electromagnetic waves were superimposed. This caused interference which was then used to extract information. "Where is it?" he mumbled under his breath, starting to get frustrated.

He knew finding that number was integral to the rest of the puzzle: how and where the information was being sent. When he finally located it, he looked up the company that made the device and saw the price tag, suggesting that he was dealing with someone who had deep pockets and solidifying his suspicions that this was a formidable enemy. "Thirty-two thousand dollars? You've got to be kidding me," he exclaimed out loud. "Who has that kind of money to blow on a small-town security operation? Unless it's not a small issue."

James put the microphone inside the pocket of one of his duffle bags. He was curious to find out who planted the device and who was monitoring the transmissions. He was glad for the notes he had taken in his coded journal. Figuring all that out would take some time, but it would have to wait. Supper was starting in a few minutes and James knew he had to maintain his schedule to keep up appearances now that he was being monitored closer than he had ever realized. He understood that any deviation would be noticed and raise suspicions. Plus, he was hungry.

James contemplated the fact that the more he learned about the anomalies in this Ebola response, the less he knew who he could trust. Stepping into that dining room seemed even more like a minefield than it had on previous evenings. He had to be more cautious and less chatty. Plus, each word he spoke needed to be precisely planned both to protect his intel as well as his ability to gain more insight from the answers and responses of others. With this new awareness, James navigated through supper conversations with rigor and returned to his room to figure out who his true enemies were on this mission.

Chapter 39

James decided to make sure that his laptop was not being surveiled. There was no sense in using it to research the laser microphone if that medium was unsecure. He took a few minutes to run a back-door search for any unusual viruses and was relieved to discover none.

Taking out the piece of paper where he had written the serial number for that particular model, he wanted to know how the information was most likely to be accessed. His question was whether the data would have been communicated to a simple monitor, similar to a baby monitor, or if it had been sent via a more sophisticated means like software to another laptop.

According to the manufacturer's specs, the microphone did come with a software program that allowed the data it collected to be transferred via WiFi to one or more laptops. It was supported by a CAD system, used to improve communications in the device creating the form of electronic files for print. Now that James knew what he was dealing with, his next step was to find out who had employed it to spy on him and why.

He already had a short list of suspects; people whose intentions he had a difficult time deciphering, like Jim Pressman, J.P. Walker, and the mystery man. And, honestly, Victor was someone he could not figure out. His family connections could make him as tainted as the rest, but James' gut was telling him that he could be trusted. He decided that talking to Victor at breakfast in the morning would be vital to nailing down his enemy.

James would need help tracing the microphone to the transmission source and believed Caleb would be able to assist him, or at least point him toward someone who could. His field of expertise was communication, but not necessarily computers. He needed someone who could trace the transmission backwards and pinpoint an exact receiver.

James did one more sweep of his room, took one last trip to the WC, and tucked himself into his netting with his journal of coded notes, paper, cell phone, flashlight, and water. His plan was to thoroughly think through his suspicions, but fatigue overcame him. Within twenty minutes, he was out.

With so much on his mind, however, he didn't sleep long. James pulled himself out of bed and did his typical routine, but remembering Victor's hint about a good place to start in understanding the elusive enemy, he then returned to his room and began to do some research on his laptop. *The Georgia Guidestones, eh?* James thought as he punched the term into the search bar. *Seems like I've heard of them but never more than a passing phrase or comment. What are you?*

Of course, he went first to a basic report on the structure, who built it, and why. James was intrigued by the idea that the funders were anonymous, and that the front man who paid for the project used the pseudonym, Robert C. Christian. When he read through the ten guidelines, his first thought was that the wording sounded a bit like something the Founding Fathers would use, like tempered reason, a concept promoted by Benjamin Franklin and Thomas Jefferson, and probably many others. But he figured his talk with Victor that morning would likely only center around the first two guidelines: having the population of humanity under five hundred million and the wise guidance of reproduction.

James suddenly remembered something Julia had said, and Victor had confirmed, about new contraceptives that were often tested among the women of African nations. Some women were still being given an under-the-skin method that was facing lawsuits in the United States for serious side effects. He clicked his laptop closed, locked his door, and headed to the cafeteria.

No matter how early he thought he would be, James always found Victor in the dining room before he arrived. It was really nice to have an early bird for a friend. Victor rose as he greeted James. "I know handshakes are not permitted but..." James chuckled as the two men gave each other a side-hug and hearty pats on one another's backs.

"Hey," James said, cutting right to the chase, "I may break my normal routine and chat with you first while this place is completely empty. Do you mind? Were you in the middle of something?"

"Of course not. But at least go grab a drink before you sit down."

James quickly filled a glass of water, snagged a piece of bread, and returned to a chair directly across from Victor; he needed a good view of his face to study him while he was answering.

"So, what's on your mind?"

"I feel like a lot has happened since our last hearty conversation," James began. "But I wanted to pick up on that discussion that started when J.P. was sitting with us that one morning. You mentioned the Georgia Guidestones and that I needed to do my homework, which I did only in the last hour. What's your opinion on the set of ten guidelines? Is it something to be taken seriously?" James paused, expecting an answer from Victor but didn't get one. "I guess what I'm asking is, bottom line, should I be worried about what is engraved on those stones as part of my security assignment here?"

Victor began his response with a steady look at the floor for a brief moment. When he lifted his head, his intense gaze scared James. "There is so much that I could tell you, but I'm bound to a certain level of secrecy. I'm torn between what is expected of me and my respect for you. But let me start by saying that you should take the first guideline very seriously. That number, five hundred million, has been studied for years by experts who feel that is the best population for maintaining life on this planet. And yes, I do believe that it should be foundational to your decisions here in this crisis response."

"What I find appalling," James continued, shaking his head, "is the arrogance that would suggest that billions of people should be eliminated. I know I'm repeating myself, but who gets to decide that? Again, it sounds like playing God to me. I just can't wrap my mind around it."

"You better," Victor said.

James let out a deep sigh. "Do you think something like an unchecked disease would be utilized to achieve these goals?"

"Again, I'm going to defer on giving you direct answers," Victor confessed. "Remember that I am caught between my own conscience, your conscience, and the expectations of my family. What I think is right is irrelevant to this conversation, James. You have to remember that."

"That's it?" James asked incredulously, expecting more from his friend.

"For the answer as to the person setting the criteria for who should survive and who should be eliminated, I'm giving you another homework assignment. Study eugenics. That field was well-documented in Germany during World War II."

"You're killing me, Victor. Instead of giving me direct answers, you just keep throwing me teasers that feel like delay tactics."

"But I'm not. I'm sincerely trying to help you the only way I can."

"The only way you can?" James barked. "What does that mean? Is that because of your obligation to secrecy? You're scaring me, man. You've got me thinking that we're talking about some kind of crazy conspiracy theory that might actually be, not only true, but working toward a global holocaust bigger than anything anyone could have ever imagined."

"Except the people who already have." Victor's solemn statement was met by a stunned silence. "Listen," he eventually continued, "I promised to have your back as much as is in my power, but you cannot ask me to break protocol when it comes to my family's expectations. I cannot directly answer your questions. All I can do is point you in the right direction. And, remember, it's only a conspiracy theory until you find out it's an actual conspiracy." Victor gave James a wink to try and ease the tension before attempting to switch subjects. "By the way, how is that Indian motorcycle coming along? Can I help you with any of the repairs? I know something of mechanics. Plus, I want you to have as many resources at your fingertips as possible. Not only equipment, but people. A whole network in your back pocket."

"Well, honestly, that bike project is mostly just a distraction, but if you actually think it could be an asset, I'd appreciate the help. I hope to have time to work on it this afternoon, if the parts arrive. Do you think you'll be available?"

Victor nodded. "I should be."

"Great," James responded. "I'll keep you posted." He stood, refilled his plate, and headed to his typical corner of the room.

Chapter 40

Each day, or even hour, instead of finding more answers and more peace, James saw problems compounding. What started as a nagging feeling in his gut was now a full-fledged emergency. He could barely keep his mind focused. He sat down and let his head drop. For at least a full five minutes, he just stared at the floor. Then he closed his eyes and followed his own advice drawn from years of training as a Special Forces soldier.

He breathed in deep, sat up straight, and stretched out his shoulder and back muscles. With his eyes still closed, he breathed out a whispered prayer. "O God, I am so scared right now. Please grant me Your wisdom. Lend me Your support in all the ways You see I need it. Show me who the enemy is in this place. Protect the response team. Protect this village and nation. Protect me and, God, please return me safely to my family who I am so grateful for." James paused as a sob caught his throat. He sat still for several minutes before opening his eyes, drawing his Bible toward him, and preparing his journal. With pen in hand, he went straight to Psalm twenty-seven and read the whole thing. Reading it a second time, he underlined phrases and prayed promises back to God, making them specific to his situation. "LORD, set me up on a rock; lift up my head above my enemies that surround me. Let me know who planted that microphone and where the transmission is going. Strengthen me against the attacks of an unknown enemy, and the ones that are obvious like J.P. I promise that I will sing Your praises when you deliver me."

When James finished the prayer, he felt calmer, and his mind was super sharp and focused. He immediately decided to list his best assets and resources, starting with the people on the property who he believed that he could trust: Victor, Lucas, Kongolo, as well as Katey and his brother. From the village, he wrote down Amin and David. Then he thought about a wider security net. He would need to call Julia and have her ask Wesley for his best contacts in Kinshasa and around the Congo. Her brother-in-law's years in the diamond industry had given him the opportunity to make solid, influential friends which could prove to be beneficial in the future.

James also listed those he could rely on outside of Congo: his parents, Julia and her family, his pastor, Caleb and all of the guys from his old unit. He pondered Colonel Fitzpatrick for a second but decided to trust others through Caleb and his suggestions instead.

He felt like he needed information specific to his mission. The time had come, he was going to enter the dark web that night and look for information on this particular outbreak. He needed to know what he was up against.

James was glad to be writing all of this in his code because earlier than typical, J.P. entered the cafeteria. She gave him only a cursory glance, then headed straight for Victor, sitting down close to him in that familiar way. The proximity made Victor uncomfortable, which was obvious as he attempted to scoot himself in the opposite direction.

In his observation, James wondered if all that Victor had said about her was true, and his assumptions based upon those statements were accurate. Was she really there to sabotage the response? Who would send her on such a mission, and what would cause her to agree to it? Was the old money these families came from involved? Was he even safe? These were questions that needed to be answered and those answers needed to come sooner rather than later. Before he fully completed the list he was working on, James started an additional list of suspects. He placed Jim Pressman and J.P. Walker at the top, in code of course.

Within a few minutes, others began to trickle into the cafeteria, and soon the room was three quarters full. James looked up and smiled at Lucas as he sat down. They exchanged good-mornings and plowed into the main breakfast but kept the conversation light. Neither wanted to spoil the morning with what weighed heavily on their minds. James finished and dismissed himself. He returned to his room to plan his survival strategy.

Chapter 41

Kongolo had watched the whole cafeteria of international response workers as they ate their breakfast while he prepared for his day. He particularly kept his eye on J.P. and Victor, and then James as well. From his position behind the counter, sorting through beans for the next day's meal, he wanted to gauge the attitudes of people in the room and observe any danger that might present itself to James. He felt so indebted to that man for rescuing him and his sister and giving them back their lives. As far as he was concerned, James' safety was vital. Knowing that James was already worried about J.P., keeping an eye on her would be a secondary task for his day.

He had seen James get up and leave the room and saw J.P. follow him with her eyes. A moment later she gave Pressman a look that raised Kongolo's suspicions. He watched her leave the room and, three minutes later, so did Pressman. Kongolo knew he needed to monitor the situation, so he told the kitchen boss had to use the WC.

Walking out the side door of the kitchen, he decided to follow the footpath that lined the back side of the long, two-story building. Slowing down and carefully peeking around the corner, he looked first to the left to be sure no one was tracking him and then to the right toward the press dorm and the bathroom area behind it.

He drew back imperceptibly when he saw Pressman, J.P., and a third person talking behind the first shower room. They seemed to be engrossed in their conversation. Pressman was the only one glancing around, but never in Kongolo's direction. Kongolo was close enough to know that they were speaking English, but too far to make out many of the words. He decided to record the conversation on his phone, hoping to capture something that would help James.

He kept waiting for the third man to turn around long enough to give Kongolo a glimpse of his face, but the man seemed purposefully careful to look away from the main area of the campus.

He must be the gopher of the group.

Although one would think that Pressman would be leading the meeting, it was clear to any observer that J.P. was definitely the one in charge.

As his phone continued to record, Kongolo caught a few heated words from J.P.'s raised voice. "What are we going to do with this James guy? I mean, his life is as quaint as the lyrics to a country-western song. Seriously, how am I supposed to seduce a man like that?"

"Lower your voice," Kongolo heard Pressman respond. "You were brought here with that one task. Do not mess it up!" He turned to the other man and continued, "What have you learned about the halted transmission from James' room? Is the device still in position?" Kongolo could not hear the response, but he hoped the phone was picking it up. The man turned just enough for Kongolo to notice the cleft in his chin. He ducked back to be sure he wasn't seen but then decided that he had been away from his job long enough and better return before his absence became suspect.

He texted James on the way back saying that they needed to rendezvous as soon as possible to discuss what he had just witnessed. James asked him to meet by the newly installed chain-link fence along the back perimeter of the property in ten minutes. When that time came, Kongolo excused himself again, saying he had stomach issues; a story that was not entirely false.

The two men reached the spot at almost the same time but coming from opposite directions. They met with a back-pounding hug and James jumped right into the conversation.

"So, tell me what's going on."

"After you left the cafeteria, J.P. gave Monsieur Pressman a strange look and left the room. Not long after, he also left. I excused myself to go to the WC. When I went by the backside of the long building, I saw them talking to a third man. Not being able to hear everything, I decided to use the record app on my phone to get the conversation.

I hope everything is on this. Your concerns were rightly placed. I think J.P. is your main problem."

"Let's have a listen to that recording," James answered. Most of it was too quiet to pick up full sentences, but the few words and phrases that were clear were significant. And when J.P. had raised her voice, both men knew exactly what kind of person they were dealing with.

The rest of the conversation that was audible was obviously a discussion about James and how they were to deal with the threat that he posed to their true mission there in Domiongo and Congo. But J.P.'s comment about being only on the grounds to seduce James made him shiver despite the heat and humidity of early morning in the tropics. He was scared. His voice felt strained as he spoke.

"Listen, Kongolo, I need you to keep this between us for now. Will you please email that recording to me? I want to share it with a few friends that I can trust, both here in Congo and in America. If I'm going to survive and protect this response and the village, I need as much anonymity as possible."

"Sure, Monsieur," Kongolo said, "you can count on me. But first, can you show me how to email this recording?" Kongolo handed his phone to James who took it, studied the app, and had the recording sent within a few seconds. He thanked Kongolo for his foresight in following J.P. and Pressman. The men wrapped things up with another big hug and went their separate ways, both understanding how important it was to not raise any suspicions among those intent on James' demise.

Kongolo returned to his duties in the kitchen, and James headed back to his chamber to prepare for his meeting with the security team. When that was through, he wanted to work on the dirt bike. Now more than ever, he realized the wisdom of having a convenient way to escape the area if it became necessary.

Back in his room, James locked himself in and nearly fell on the floor with the weight of this new information. He was being intentionally watched. J.P. was there for the express purpose of ruining him with a strategic seduction. All throughout his military career, he had faced terrifying enemies, including those in the rebel camp six years ago which challenged every aspect of his training, but this made those experiences look like child's play. He needed to know who the true enemy was behind the surveillance and the planned seduction.

Finally, he once again calmed himself by breathing in slowly and breathing out a prayer. James counted to twenty as he inhaled. Then he slowly exhaled, "LORD, You are my light and my salvation. Reveal truth to me. Continue to be the strength of my life emotionally, spiritually, mentally, and physically. God, if You will do this for me, I know that I won't need to fear what man can do to me." He breathed in again and breathed out, "LORD, put the right people in the right places to help me do what You have called me here to do."

James lay still for several more minutes before he pulled himself off the woven mat he was on. He felt calmer and more battle ready than he did before his prayer. Knowing the seriousness of this crisis, he was fully aware that he had been placed in this situation for such a time as this.

He glanced over his notes for the security team meeting and then left, resolving to not allow all the turmoil in his heart and mind to be reflected in his countenance or attitude when he got there. He even forced himself to whistle the chorus of one of his favorite worship songs, "God of Angel Armies." The thought of an angel army as having his back even made him smile.

Chapter 42

James' meeting went off without a hitch as the team was united in their goal to secure the response and the school campus in Domiongo. The consequences of not doing their job well sobered up even the youngest among them. Plus, they all accepted James' leadership, knowing they could trust his intuition.

After lunch, Victor met James in his room to help with the Indian repairs. Parts that he had been waiting for had finally arrived on the plane from Kinshasa, along with medical and tech supplies for the response team. Both men were eager to see the bike up and running.

"Do you know what you're doing with this motorcycle?" Victor asked. "Seems like an antique would be difficult to repair."

"You would think," James replied, "but it was relatively easy to find replacement parts on Amazon. Even the spark plug, A7TC, was only eight bucks. Obviously, it cost more to have it shipped than it cost to purchase it. The other repairs were pretty much standard motorcycle mechanics. Even the tires could be replaced with a forty-five inch, similar to the one on the original 1928 Scout. Rock solid engineering to be sure. Do you know much about the history of the company?"

"Totally. Who hasn't heard of an Indian? Especially after that Anthony Hopkins movie. But, honestly, I'm not that mechanically inclined. I mean, I guess I know enough to get by."

"Well, it has a seven-fifty cc, V-twin engine. Super durable, which is apparent by the fact that an Indian from that vintage is sitting in my room today. I'm just hoping that these last few pieces will get this thing up and running."

The two men began tinkering, and while James wanted to avoid a serious conversation, he knew it was inevitable. "Victor, I have to be honest with you. The things that you've shared with me recently are quite alarming."

"They are," Victor agreed. "I've lived with stuff like this my whole life. I don't know how someone like you, hearing this all for the first time, handles it."

"Well, to tell you the truth, my natural instinct is to jump on this thing and ride off into the jungle full throttle and escape it all. But my faith allows me to live above what would otherwise come instinctively."

"Is that for real?" Victor questioned before adding, "How do you know that you can count on it the way you do? Aren't you afraid of being wrong? Of simply trusting in a fairy tale?"

"First of all, I don't get the problem people have with fairy tales. They're often based on actual historical events, like Snow White and Rose Red. They endure for good reason and often reveal beautiful, deep truths."

"Valid points," Victor started, "but still..."

"Right. Back to my faith, which is no fairy tale, by the way. I owe Jesus everything. What I experienced in Eastern Congo six years ago was truly a nightmare, and I couldn't have surived it without Him."

"Tell me."

"You already know some of the story," James began. "I had inadvertently met up with Julia there which excited me because I had been into her in high school, but then we lost touch and I had never stopped thinking about her. Then we were abducted by that small rebel group and I was terrified. What I knew would happen to her if I was killed still haunts me. Plus, the physical trauma of that event has never been fully erased. I've been seeing a counselor these past few years simply because I've never been able to completely let go, and my mental health is a critical component to my relationship with my family."

"Yeah, I've been wanting to hear more about that."

"Well, I was only tortured the one time," James started, "but that was enough. The fear of these last few weeks has really opened a raw spot in my mind. I've clung to Jesus for six years, but I feel like I have never leaned on His wisdom so desperately as I am for this mission. What else can I say?"

They worked and continued to plunk around various subjects but frequently came back to God and family. An hour before supper, the two felt as if the task was finished, but a test drive would be needed to confirm it. James did not want to start it up in the compound and draw unnecessary attention to himself, so they agreed to meet at the front gate at eight o'clock. They parted at James' door, both looking forward to the ride.

Chapter 43

James had given himself one task before the appointment to test the Indian: getting onto the dark web to explore any articles about the current Ebola outbreak. Although he was a communications specialist and had been trained in layers of internet content, he had never actually taken the plunge. But he knew enough to use the proper channels.

He decided early on to use TOR, an acronym meaning The Onion Router, which referred to the various layers keeping the average surfer from entering damaging domains. TOR was created to give anyone the freedom to explore the internet without being placed under surveillance or scammed. Using this service's multi-layer encryption process, James soon found himself looking for articles and information about Ebola in general and this outbreak specifically.

As he browsed through different sites, he took notes using his simple code, wanting to be able to come back later and peruse the information. He saw nothing shocking or out of the ordinary until he came to one site that seemed to be originating somewhere in Israel, since the information had first been written in Hebrew and then translated. He found a couple of things that scared him. The intel hinted that the rights to the Ebola virus actually belonged to one group, primarily controlled by a family whose name James had quite recently become very familiar with. It was also inferred that this outbreak may have been purposefully started with the intent of observing how quickly it could spread if certain protocols were not carefully followed.

James could hardly breathe, but when he did, he could feel his chest tighten with the intensity of the choking fear that welled up in him. He wanted to click his laptop shut and get himself on the first plane home. But he didn't, realizing that he was in too deep and that he was already invested in his mission to secure this response. Knowing and loving people in the area that would need his protection and be defenseless if he deserted them, he was determined to stay and see this thing through.

James looked around the article a bit more, sending a message that requested the contributor reach out to him with any other information. He had created a new email account just for this purpose. He shut his computer to get ready for his test drive, but his mind was stuck. Stuck on the danger involved in his continuing on with this mission. He could hardly believe what he had just learned but was forced to accept it due to Victor's own cryptic warnings. The urgency for survival while protecting his colleagues and the Congolese in that area had never weighed heavier. As ready as he could be, he clicked off the overhead light and opened the door.

James took a minute to see if there were any Westerners nearby and was pleased to find there was actually no one in sight. He stepped back into his room, grabbed the bike, and quickly rolled it around the end of the building to the right. As he went back to lock his door, he caught a glimpse of Victor rounding the corner of the press dorm in the direction of the shower.

The two men met up and silently walked the bike down a little-known path in the direction of the front gate. James left the bike a second with Victor while he chatted with the sentinel. When he returned, it only took them a moment to get the bike outside.

James was thankful he had replaced the original headlight with a new kit that included a brighter bulb as the darkness of their surroundings was intense. They pushed the bike two hundred meters south toward the village, and James straddled the seat. Victor held a flashlight to make it even easier to see.

"Give it a kick, James. I'm as eager to find out if this bike runs as you are. If it needs tweaking, let's get on with it."

James placed his right foot on the kickstart that he had already positioned. He lifted his foot up and pressed down with all the force in his right leg. The bike sputtered but stopped. Again, he gave it everything he had, but this time the bike came to life under him, still choking and gasping, but not stalling.

"That's a good sign, James," Victor encouraged. "At least it's going. Take it down the path a bit and see how it steers and turns." With that, James guided it in the direction of the north part of the village, loving the stability of the bike's ride but worrying about the continued sputtering. He turned it around and drove back to Victor.

"Give it a spin, bro. Let me know what you think," James offered. "I'm wondering if I got the mixture of the oil and gas wrong."

"Possible, but that's an easy fix," Victor said as he climbed onto the ancient machine. Like James, he took off in the direction of the town but rode further. Once he had the bike back to the starting point, he dismounted and put down the kick stand. "This is great. You've got yourself a solid resource that could really come in handy."

James agreed heartily, though any conceivable situation that could cause him to need it terrified him. The two men stealthily pushed the Indian back to the main gate. They were let in with just a word by the sentinel who was already sworn to keep the events a secret. Once the bike was safely back in James' room, the two men parted for the night and promised to talk more in the morning. James entered his dwelling feeling better than when he had left, and he hoped that would translate into a peaceful night of sleep.

Chapter 44

Being the dry season, no rain was expected, but the day dawned cool and overcast. James loved the damp, dreary feel because it reminded him of home back in Washington State. That thought led him to reflect on Julia and the boys. He cleared his throat several times to get rid of those choking sobs that seemed to regularly haunt him these past few days. Preparing for the events that would follow, he headed to breakfast with his typical morning gear.

Despite their later-than-usual excursion, Victor had still managed to beat him to the cafeteria. The two gave each other a knowing look and said good morning. James loaded his bread plate, fixed his drinks, and decided to pause a moment for a quick chat before proceeding to his typical spot.

"How are you?" James asked. "Sleep okay? Wake up good?"

"Treating me to a traditional Lingala greeting?" Victor teased. "I slept well. I felt a bit of peace after that bike fired up."

"Oh, yeah..." James agreed with a relieving sigh. "Me, too."

"Any more thoughts on getting that oil and gas mixed right? Bet it's something that can be looked up pretty easily."

"I'm sure that it is. I just haven't had a chance yet but will make it a priority."

The two continued in brief casual conversation, but before leaving, James felt led to ask Victor if he would be open to receiving a Scripture or two. If so, James said he would text him a couple of his favorite passages. Surprisingly, Victor agreed with more enthusiasm than James would have expected. He smiled and said that he would, then left his friend to finish his breakfast in his usual place, feeling quite encouraged.

Slowly, the room began to fill up. Kongolo greeted James from the kitchen window. Pressman and Lucas soon joined him, and other tables were half full. James went to load up some more bread and refill his water and coffee cups when, suddenly, internal alarm bells began to sound. Without knowing exactly where she was, James sensed her close proximity just before he physically felt J.P. brush up against his back.

Before he could react, she whispered, "I often see you sitting in here by yourself. You must be very lonely. I'll bet you miss your wife terribly. You should stop by my room tonight and let me keep you company."

James knew only the two of them could have heard her, but he still felt like every eye in the room was watching. More dangerous than the Gabon viper he encountered six years prior, this woman was pure poison, and now Kongolo had even gotten confirmation for him that her whole purpose was to seduce him.

Out of his left eye, he saw both Victor and Kongolo staring hard in his direction. "You've learned enough about me to know that I would never accept a proposition like that," James forcefully responded, just loud enough for the whole room to clearly hear.

J.P.'s complexion switched from gray to green to purple in about half of a second. Her eyes narrowed into slits. "You have no idea who I am or what I can do, but you'll soon find out."

She quickly pivoted and made a beeline for the door. Kongolo looked relieved. Victor looked worried. Pressman looked confused. But Lucas saved the day by getting to his feet, stretching his tall frame, and loudly declaring that he needed a second cup of coffee. His casual remarks broke the tension, and soon everyone was attempting to forget what they just witnessed. A few seconds later, Pressman left the room with his plate still half full. James exchanged a glance with Kongolo as he returned to his table to resume his breakfast and attempt to calm his ruffled spirit. He hated these out-of-control feelings that events on this mission kept forcing into his conscience. To make matters worse, James caught a look from Victor that he couldn't read and decided he would bring it up in their next conversation. In the meantime, he focused on chewing, swallowing, and slowly breathing both in and out. He hadn't felt such acute danger since his captivity in the rebel camp all those years ago. Admitting to himself that he would soon have to do a thorough assessment of his own mental state, he put it at the top of his morning to-do list.

James barely managed but finished his breakfast in silence with his friend Lucas thankfully standing guard. The meal seemed dry, getting caught in his throat. He knew enough about PTSD to know that this was a typical, physical reaction to an emotional trauma. The confrontation with J.P. left him feeling overwhelmed and vulnerable, both not good for a former, well-trained Special Forces soldier.

Chapter 45

James, still feeling weak from the morning's events, excused himself and went back to his room. He closed and locked his door, then dully stared at the Indian. Having it in perfect working order was a must, but his mind could not process all the steps to do so in that moment. He felt frozen, immobile.

He knew he needed to stop right then and do a mental health check. Although he mostly considered the abduction Eastern Congo as not leaving him completely scarred, he acknowledged that there were still some issues he hadn't totally conquered. If James were honest with himself, he'd have to admit that stint in the rebel camp did injure him. The fear of getting himself killed and leaving Julia alone with those cruel men still gave him nightmares. And although the beating he received there that did bring him to within an inch of his life was relatively short-lived, it was still capable of raising his blood pressure when he thought of it. This horrific event, though not the exact same scenario, had the similar element of his being responsible for a life besides his own. But, in this case, it wasn't just one life. It was many. Not only were the people on the response team his mission, but so was the safety of the village residents and even the region. Even though the danger this time was just as real as it previously had been, it was coming from a different direction. It was not a Congolese enemy but rather an unseen and still unknown enemy that lurked just outside his realm of understanding. An evil that he would need to defeat but seemed nearly undefeatable due to its immense size and power. He was terrified at his own weakness and impotence to deal with it.

James accurately analyzed himself and realized that anxiety was his most significant symptom. It created the physical response of muscle tension and even a feeling of not being strong enough to successfully secure this response. Once he correctly laid his finger on his biggest concern, he knew what to do to remedy the issue.

James closed his eyes. He focused his mind on one Scripture:

> Though I walk through the valley of the shadow of death, I will fear no evil.

Breathing in for a count of four, he held the breath for an additional four seconds and then slowly let it out while reciting that verse in his mind. Fear no evil. Fear no evil. Fear no evil. He repeated this as he slowly breathed out all the air in his lungs.

Pausing to focus on the word "evil," he surmised that the kind he was combatting was deep-rooted, ugly, and extremely powerful. He knew that alone he was not able to defeat it but was thankful the breathing had accomplished its initial goal of calming him. Moving on to a series of stretches to relax his muscles, especially those around his neck and shoulders, helped as well. He also continued to repeat Psalm 23:4. He believed he was smack dab in the middle of the valley referenced in the verse and was unable to see a way out. He could not allow fear to hamper him when he needed his strength the most.

After stretching for fifteen minutes, the muscles around his neck began to relax. He got himself to his desk, took out a permanent marker and some blank pieces of paper on which he wrote "fear no evil," and then posted them around his room to help him focus. With that same marker he wrote 23:4 on both wrists. Then, taking out his journal, he simply poured out every thought and emotion in no particular order, knowing he would come back that night or the next morning and analyze his own thoughts to organize them better. Keeping his heart, mind, and body healthy was vital, and he knew it.

He then readied himself for the regular tasks of the day. He had to forge ahead and could not let his own personal demons keep him down. Any break in his routine would draw undue attention his way. James needed to avoid that at all costs.

Chapter 46

James finished his morning duties and made it through lunch without any mishaps; although, he did think that he was being stared at by his colleagues off and on throughout the meal. Back in his room for the whole afternoon, he turned his attention to getting the gas and oil ratio perfect for the Indian. He took time to Google repair information for a 1928 model and found a gold mine of data on one website, including a tip to place a small amount of oil in the cam-case after a motor had been disassembled for repairs. The case was supposed to have been oiled before he put everything back together. Not wanting to start from scratch, James took apart a few pieces in that area, oiled them, and reassembled the motor. With that done, he turned to the second tip.

He needed to know more about the "new" mechanical oiler that had been installed on models manufactured after 1927. His '28 Scout, according to the diagram, had a test plug that was used to check oil flow; a good point to remember, but not quite the information that he was seeking. Finding a YouTube video about mixing the right amount of gas and oil for a two-stroke, he followed the specs and hoped it was right. That night, he would give it another test run. Then he'd know if it was perfected.

James texted Victor about a second trial and got a positive response. It also included an invitation to sit with him at supper and a request to bring a notebook and a pen. James appreciated the supportive gesture and felt like he would need the extra backing after that morning's trauma. Plus, he was curious about the notebook thing.

At supper, Victor opened the conversation with something that was obviously heavy on his heart. "So, you've clearly made a dangerous enemy. That woman's threat this morning needs to be taken seriously. With that in mind, I think we should put together a list of the people you can count on to have your back. Did you bring that notebook?"

James pulled out two; his small, waterproof one and a larger one. He also pulled out his journal. "Yep. Ready. Can I start by placing you at the top of my list?"

"Sure. You can, as long as I am in the picture. Remember, I've said repeatedly that my life is not really my own. I belong to my family. Their agenda is my agenda, whether I like it or not. Tell me, who else do you know that you can rely on? Especially here in Congo. Who is on the ground that can step in if needed?"

"Already started a list in here," James said, holding up the largest of his notebooks. "People in Congo that I can count on is a growing number. Right at the top of my list is Kongolo. He's the one that works here in the kitchen. Because I helped him and his sister escape from that rebel camp six years ago, I know I have his complete loyalty. I also think that I can trust Katey, his brother Paul, Amin, a storeowner in Domiongo, Lucas, and David. No one else here stands out as a clear asset. In addition, my brother-in-law, Wesley, has several contacts in Kinshasa. I've reached out to him to send me names and information for them."

"Wow! Here I was thinking that I would be giving you a great new idea, but it sounds like you're way ahead of me. Give me that book. I want to write my address in London, and the name and information for an old, trusted friend."

"Great," James responded as he handed it over to Victor.

"He can do almost anything. Pull any strings. He's powerful but also has a strong, moral compass. Mention my name and you can get almost anything you need."

"Sounds good. Thanks, Victor. I really appreciate this."

"No problem. After supper, I'll meet you by the gate around the same time. Does that still work?"

"Definitely," James affirmed.

The men finished the meal with small talk. Three hours later, they were pushing the Indian out of the compound gate. Once again,

James took the first spin. The bike started smoothly and practically purred under his gentle attempts to rev the engine. He took off down the path and rode a good mile before turning back. Everything felt perfect. James was excited that his pet project had resulted in the restoration of such a cool, old bike, not to mention given him his own mode of transportation, if needed.

"Sounds so much better, James."

"I agree. Take it for a spin."

Victor hopped on the bike and headed off down the path toward the village before circling back to the compound area. "You're right. Runs like a dream."

"Yup. The next thing that I need is solid saddle bags. Something made out of denim or tent canvas. I'm wondering if a seamstress in town could tackle that. I'm thinking about making a trip to the village in the next day or so for some meetings with a few officials. Want to tag along?"

Chapter 47

Early the next morning, after his shower but before heading to the cafeteria, James looked over all his notes. He then put Victor and his friend's contact information in both of his phones. He transferred everything to his waterproof notebook as well, then headed to breakfast.

In the cafeteria, he greeted Victor then started his morning alone, reading Scripture and journaling. He even plugged in his earbuds and listened to two fortifying songs, and then went back to have a short chat with Victor before people began to trickle in. They kept the conversation relatively casual. But right before they parted, Victor encouraged James to share both his contact information, as well as that of his influential friend, with Julia.

During breakfast and lunch that day, it was obvious that someone was missing. J.P. did not make an appearance at either meal, and when James made a few inquiries, no one had remembered seeing her anywhere on the campus. After lunch, James had his appointment in the village. He had called earlier that morning to set a time to discuss updates with Jean Muya, the chief, and very much looked forward to the meeting since they hadn't had any contact since the night of the riot.

Katey's brother met James and Victor at the front gate at 1:30. James was sorely tempted to take his own motorcycle, but he really wanted to keep that asset a secret for as long as possible. Paul dropped the men off at a small café in town where the rendezvous was to take place. James felt like a public meeting would show solidarity between his mission and the chief's desire to keep his villagers safe. Plus, it was a perk that the café sold delicious French fries and ice-cold sodas. James ordered two fries and two Cokes, feeling the need to treat his soul to a small bit of American culture. He treated Victor to the same. Within five minutes, the chief arrived in his older Mercedes sedan and parked on the road. James rose to welcome him.

"Chief Jean," James began, "I am so glad that you agreed to meet me. I hope you don't mind if I brought my new friend along. This is Victor Archer, a reporter for SkyNews in London. Do you think we will need an interpreter? I thought between my limited Lingala and French, and your better English, that we could manage."

"I understand and speak English very well," the chief proudly stated. "I went to school on an American mission compound where it was a required course of study."

"Great."

The chief did not waste any time. "How are things going at the compound? Any new updates? Anything that you are worried about?"

"Actually, yes. There are several things that have me very concerned." James then told him about the young man at the clinic who had been given permission to sell medicines on the black market, and a description of the man with the cleft chin. James connected this event to the occurrences of broken medical protocol. Sharing about the surveillance device from his room, and Kongolo's overhearing about JP's mission, he finished with telling what happened with J.P. in the cafeteria.

"These are very grave pieces of information, indeed. What is your conclusion? Do you really believe that the response mission could be sabotaged?"

"I do," James affirmed.

"If this is true," the chief continued, "then our whole village, perhaps even the entire region could be in danger. I am very worried, my friend. But I am glad that you have shared this with me. Do you have allies on the compound or even in the country who can help you?"

"I have several close by. I'm grateful that I can add you to that list. Back in America, I have a comrade, a former soldier who knows of the issues. Plus, I have a list of contacts from my brother-in-law who worked in Congo many years. Most of which, though, live in Kinshasa. But he assures me that I can call upon them for any help."

"All very good," Jean agreed. "Is there any way to verify your suspicions?"

"I'm still working on that," James replied. "What do you suggest? How do you think I should proceed?"

"The very first thing is to confirm your intuitions from an outside source. Is there a way to find someone who knows enough about such an agenda?"

"Well, yes. At least, I think so," James answered. "I did some online research and found an article that implied that this response was a coverup or front. I reached out to the author of that article, but I am still waiting to hear back."

"Good," Jean encouraged.

"Once I hear from him, I believe that I will have the needed confirmation. But then what?"

"This is a dilemma," Jean agreed.

James continued, "How am I to complete my mission to secure the response and the compound without sticking to the written mandates? Pressman, whom I do not trust, is supposed to get weekly updates from me, but I have shared none of this with him. Any thoughts?"

"James, you must remember," Chief Jean said, "that your first mission is security. I know that you are a Christian. I have heard this spoken of in the village. That means you are a praying man. You must continually ask God to give you wisdom to complete your duty to keep the people on the compound, and ultimately the village, safe. This is more important than answering to a man you do not trust. I am not saying to lie, but I am advising simply that you not share everything you know. If you don't trust this man, he may be a part of a sabotage plan."

"Thank you," James said, breathing a sigh of relief. "I agree, and it helps to hear it from someone of your position."

"What is next?"

"Well, I will continue in my post and do everything in my power to gather the truth. I promise to keep you informed. I will not leave the region without some sort of plan to protect both the compound and the village. You have my word on that."

"Merci. I truly appreciate your spirit and your commitment to keeping to your mission. I understand that you have a family and so your dedication is truly a sacrifice. On behalf of my village, I thank you."

Before the two finished their conversation, James asked the chief if he could recommend a quality tailor in the village. Jean pointed him in the direction of the main market and told him to locate a mama named Odette. The men parted, promising to stay in daily contact by text or phone.

James and Victor found Odette's booth, and with the help of a young teen, managed to clearly express the dimensions of the saddlebags needed for the Indian. They agreed on both a price and a day to pick up the completed project. James gave her half the money and promised to bring the rest when he came to pick them up. He and Victor made their way back to the compound. James' stomach churned in response to the dread as he walked through the front gate, almost as if he were walking into his own prison cell. His skin crawled as the gate shut behind him, and he was filled with an intense terror that he was not able to shake.

Chapter 48

James decided to call a post-breakfast meeting with his trusted friends to discuss the latest concerns. Victor, Lucas, Katey, and Kongolo gathered in the empty sitting room. He wanted their input into the true nature of the security related to the response mission. Those who were not present were deliberately left out.

"Good morning," James began. "I hope this meeting will be productive. Victor, you are here mostly in the capacity of a friend, although some things that we discuss may potentially be intel you could use in a report later. Plus, your experience and knowledge could provide some valuable context for what we're discussing. Lucas, I'm counting on you for insight into the impact of the disease. I know we're having an open conversation here, but I don't want that to be mistaken for freedom to share what we discuss with anyone else, either here on the compound, or even in the village. Are we all in agreement on this?"

They all nodded. Victor wrote a short note as James opened the meeting up for discussion. "Let's start with everybody just voicing what their biggest concerns are right now. We'll begin with Lucas, then go around the circle."

"I have many concerns," Lucas began, "so narrowing it to my biggest is tough, but I would have to say the main one is the lack of progress with controlling the outbreak. It feels like a wildfire that is only ten percent contained. Besides, the resources and personnel are being placed at risk with almost no results. I have a family, as do many others here. Risking losing my life and leaving my wife and kids just to end up failing is really weighing on my mind. It's just not worth it," Lucas finished with a sigh.

"What do you mean by only ten percent contained?" Victor asked. "Is it normal for an outbreak like this to be rated like a forest fire?"

"In a way, yes. After the Liberian outbreak a few years past, a strategy was created with the acronym RITE, the Rapid Isolation and Treatment of Ebola. Using this, other response teams have had notable success in slowing the death rate and stopping the spread of the disease. By rapidly isolating and treating cases, it's halted quickly. Part of what I do outside of the clinic every week is write what's called an MMWR, the Morbidity and Mortality Weekly Report, which should be showing a lower death rate and a shorter chain of transmission. Less people should be contracting the disease each week, but that's just not happening. The percentage of defeating this enemy should be increasing, but I'm not seeing that. Actually, the rate of new cases has slightly increased since I have been here."

"Why do you think this is so?" Katey asked, chiming in.

"That's just it," Lucas replied, "I can't put my finger on it. Although we are all following the proven protocols, the disease is not being contained. I just don't understand."

Kongolo and James exchanged glances and then looked at Victor. The three of them stared at each other for several seconds without saying anything. Finally, James spoke up. "Yeah, Lucas, that is a big concern. Although, I have my suspicions about the reasons, I don't know how much should be shared right now." Turning to address the whole group, he continued. "Lucas knows things that he has only shared with me. The same is true of Victor and Kongolo, and I know one important fact that the rest of you are not yet privy to." James quickly glanced around, beyond the group, to be sure no one was within ear shot before asking, "Shall we be completely open?"

"We're already placing ourselves in a position of compromise by sitting here," Victor asserted. "I believe that we should be fully transparent. We've already sworn ourselves to discretion."

"All right," James affirmed before turning to Kongolo to get the ball rolling. "Go ahead and share with the others what you overheard J.P. saying about me two days ago."

Kongolo recounted the details of hearing J.P., Pressman, and a third man discussing the fact that J.P.'s express task was to seduce James in an attempt to hamper his mission of securing the response team. Everyone who wasn't already aware of this gave a long, low whistle. James nodded his affirmation and reminded everyone of what happened in the cafeteria, adding the quiet words that J.P. had spoken in his ear.

"That is scary," Victor said, with Lucas agreeing. "I know this woman by reputation and warned James about her a week ago."

"Lucas, can you share what we discovered about the cause in the breach of protocol?"

Lucas told the story about the young man selling medication out the back door of the clinic and gave his description of the unknown stranger who asked him to do it as having a cleft in his chin. This made Kongolo start.

"That man that I saw with J.P. and Monsieur Pressman also had this," Kongolo added, mimicking a cleft in his chin with his finger. James added that the same feature was on the face of the man he chased after catching him peek in his window. He then told of finding the device that was surveilling his room.

The pieces were starting to come together. Everyone was already on highly alert, but what Katey said next made their blood drain from their faces.

"These are all very serious concerns, and my report is also bad news. My brother Paul overheard in the market about some young men speaking of attacking the next burial team. I know that bodies of people who die from Ebola must be buried properly to prevent spread of the disease, but families of the deceased also desire to follow their own traditions. They are willing to go to any lengths to honor their dead. I have no details, but I will continue to search them out."

"And adding to all this is the death of the lesula and the riot at the gate," Victor stated, seeking the reassurance that only leadership could provide. "Things are not sounding very good, my friend. What should we do?"

All the men stared at James, waiting for an answer. But he just didn't have one.

Chapter 49

James shrugged his shoulders, sighed, and felt an overwhelming sense of doom blanket him as he faced his friends. He had no answers, so he offered what he knew was best.

"Not that we haven't been doing this all along, but I think that we should pray about what is going on here. Let's ask for wisdom, revealing of truth, and guidance on how to best fulfill our mission to keep this compound and village safe." Everyone around him indicated they agreed, so James began.

"Father, I am so scared. You know this. You've watched the terror in my heart gradually grow stronger since I landed here three weeks ago. I am almost continuously gripped in this prison of trepidation. Father, You are a Warrior, much more skilled than I am. Show me, show us, Your way forward. Give us the wisdom of Daniel and the courage of David. Amen."

Lucas picked up the prayer for wisdom, especially in his field of medicine. He also confessed his fear of not seeing his family again. He prayed for James before Kongolo and Katey offered their prayers for wisdom and protection. When it came to Victor, he passed but joined in at the end with a hearty "amen."

The group broke up to head to their duties, but all went with a renewed sense of being capable, through God's help, of defeating this known enemy of Ebola and the unknown one that they couldn't quite identify. They promised to meet on Sunday morning for a bit of worship.

James went back to his room to call Julia. He wanted her fully aware of the situation of things on the ground, and especially wanted to share about the experience with J.P. He was worried that a social media scandal would be created and reach her that way before he could share it.

He dialed her number, knowing that it was late the night before in Washington state. He hoped that he wasn't waking Julia, who was an early-to-bed girl. He smiled at the thought as he heard the click he was anticipating.

"Hello? James?"

"Hey, Babe. Were you asleep?"

"No, I was just lying in bed reading. Is everything okay?"

"Yeah, I guess. I wanted to touch base with you about some developments. Things here seem to be slipping out of my hands. I hate to say this out loud, but I will need to rely more on God and less on my own skills and experience for this one."

"Well, now I'm nervous. Tell me what's going on."

James shared with her about the dead lesula and his suspicions that it was used for testing. He then explained about the near riot outside the compound gate, about finding the surveillance device, and the late-night peeping Tom. He continued with Kongolo's overhearing about J.P. being sent to sabotage him and finished with the story of the confrontation in the cafeteria and her sudden absence that followed.

"Julia, this woman scares me more than all the other events combined. To know that I have been targeted has me shook. I think I'm in way over my head here."

"Who wouldn't be?" Julia added in a supportive tone.

"I think this outbreak and response are being controlled by bigger powers than even the disease itself."

"Sounds like it."

James continued, "I want you to be assured that everything that happened with J.P. was all out in the open. Everyone in that lunchroom saw how it went down."

Julia breathed out slowly but couldn't keep her voice from quivering as she spoke. "James, you know I trust you. So, no worries on that front. But I am concerned about your being targeted. It means that you are not only in danger from the disease, but also from someone or something so powerful it might be worse."

James agreed, expressed his love and devotion for her and the boys, and confirmed that surviving this mission was his top priority. However, he also admitted that he had to focus on protecting not only the compound but the entire village. He then asked Julia to get everyone she knew praying without sharing any of it on social media and explained that he couldn't risk anyone involved knowing what he suspected.

They sat silently on the phone for several minutes. Both trying to control their tears. Both reaching around the globe in an attempt to comfort and strengthen the other. Eventually, they said a simple goodbye and hung up. James was worn out from the emotions dredged up by that call. Julia laid awake for hours. Deep love often causes a couple to suffer the most during seasons of separation and hardship. But for Julia, the added element of danger and the very real possibility that James might not make it home, made it even worse.

Chapter 50

James had commissioned Victor to ask Pressman about J.P.'s sudden absence under the guise of a report he was working on but, unfortunately, that proved futile. Victor said that Pressman never responded definitively to any questions and that even his expression gave nothing away.

Despite the typical dry season mornings of mist and cool breezes, James awoke to a clear Sunday and looked forward to gathering with his friends for worship. At 9:00 a.m. he took his Bible, journal, pen, and phone to the meeting room. He had researched a few well-known worship songs that he wanted them to sing. Pierre, the Congolese doctor, tagged along when he greeted James and found where he was headed. Although James welcomed Pierre for worship, he knew that the group could not speak as freely as they had a few days ago.

Everyone else was already there. Lucas, Victor, Kongolo, and Katey were sitting in a messy circle, made possible by a few chairs and small couches being pulled around a coffee table on which Lucas had propped up his feet. James smirked. *Are only Americans that comfortable with their furniture to put their feet up on it?* he wondered.

James greeted everyone and then addressed the obvious fact that there was a newcomer. "I hope you don't mind Pierre being here. He stopped me as I was crossing the courtyard and asked if he could join us."

"Fine with us," Victor answered for all as everyone else simply nodded their welcome.

James introduced the songs that he had picked on YouTube. Those with smart phones opened right to the first one, but those without them were forced to share with their neighbors. James had chosen In Christ Alone and God of Angel Armies. Lucas knew both well, so he and James led the group. Victor picked them up quickly and sang along. The Congolese stumbled at first but were soon belting out the words to the best of their abilities. James asked Kongolo to lead them in Yesu, Ndeko Na Bolingo, the local version of What a Friend We Have in Jesus. Only James and the Congolese men knew the words by heart. It was an emotional moment and James noticed that Kongolo teared up as he was singing.

As the last line was sung, the room went quiet. Kongolo finally broke the silence. "James, that was the song that your Julia sang to start the events that freed us from the rebel camp. Do you remember?"

"Yes," James replied. "That's why I know it so well and why I chose it. It means so much to me. And obviously to you, too. I am so glad, for both of us, we made it out of there alive." He cleared his throat several times to loosen his choking emotions.

James then led the group to discuss David's defeat of Goliath. He had deliberately chosen the account because of the dire predicament that they were all in, and he intentionally emphasized the hope of the message within the story. No matter how powerful the enemy, no matter how insurmountable the odds, God can do anything that He wills through a cooperative and humble person. Victor hung on every word with bated breath and had several questions when James opened the lesson up for discussion.

"Do you think that God is capable of defeating any giant? Even a supremely powerful one?"

Lucas looked at James. "I'd like to jump in on this one." James gestured the go-ahead and Lucas turned to Victor. "God is more powerful than any other creature or organization in the universe. As Creator, He is by default stronger than any aspect of His creation. How could He be God if He could create something larger than Himself?"

"I see your point," Victor stated, hesitantly. "Still, there are families and organizations out there that are beyond anything you've ever imagined."

Kongolo jumped in, "Monsieur Victor, I know that God can do

anything. And I am sure that He can use anyone to do His work. Six years ago, I was forced to be a juvenile soldier in a rebel camp out east. My sister was also a captive there. She had great faith and prayed for God to send someone to help us escape. He answered her prayer by sending this man to us. I am here today in this place with a wife, children, and a job because this man was the David that killed our giant of captivity and horror. Do not doubt what God can do, sir."

James dropped his gaze at Kongolo's words. Sometimes, the trauma of that short captivity shook him to his core. He spent years trying to exorcise that "what if" demon from his mind. All the things that could have gone wrong continued to haunt him.

Victor noticed his friend's reaction and laid a hand on his shoulder. "What is your answer? I'm sure that you believe God can do anything."

"I do," James said.

Victor still was not convinced. "So, you really think that God could save me and free me from the entanglement of my family? You know enough to understand how difficult that would be."

James responded with an intense look. "Of course. There are a lot of things that are impossible on our own strength, but *all* things are possible with God...including saving your soul. That would be relatively easy."

"How easy?"

James explained, "You just need to accept that everything you've done wrong has been taken away by Jesus' death, burial, and resurrection. However, extracting yourself from those other expectations may be your own personal Goliath to defeat. But you can do it, with God's help. I really do believe that."

Victor looked gravely around and slowly nodded his head in agreement. "Okay. I think I want to do this. I've known for a long time I had to get out from under the bondage of my past. This is what I've needed all along. Thank you, James. Your life has impacted mine more than you'll ever know."

The whole group was sobered by this announcement and gathered around to pray for him, but only James was privy to enough information about his new friend to realize just how monumental of a decision it was.

Pressman happened past the room as the men were praying for Victor. He grimaced, clearly not happy with what he saw. Kongolo caught his disapproval but turned his face away to avoid being noticed. He immediately planned to tell James when he had the opportunity.

The men finished praying, but no one was eager to part for their separate duties, so they stayed and continued to discuss the response. Lucas brought up the need to follow proper protocol when burying those who died from the disease, but also reiterated the fear brought on by the villagers and their desire to honor customs. James asked a few key questions to assess the danger and assured Lucas that he would be on hand to secure the ceremony. Katey also promised men to help.

The conversation was interrupted by James' cell phone ringing. Surprised to be getting a call on a Sunday, he tentatively answered. "Hello?"

"Hello, James. This is Amin. I am sorry to bother you on your day of rest."

"No matter, Amin. We were just finishing our worship time. What's up?"

"I wanted you to know that I have decided to move my family to an apartment in Kinshasa. I have a cousin there who owns and rents several properties. He has one open right now, and I would feel better if my family is away from the risk of this virus."

"Okay," James responded. "How long will you be gone?"

"Only a week or two to help them get settled and get my boys into a good school. I'll be leaving on a small plane that is going to Kinshasa tomorrow. My store will remain open under the management of my sentinel. Is there anything that I can do for you while I am in the city?"

"I don't believe that I need anything, but can I call you if I think of something?"

"Yes, of course. And, please know that I am praying for you. I know I serve a different god, but it is one who also wants to see this disease eradicated. Thank you for all that you are doing for this task."

"You are welcome, Amin. Thanks both for your prayers and for informing me of your plans. I feel better knowing that your family will be secure. Take care of yourself."

James ended the call and said goodbye to his group, telling Victor that he'd be sure to sit with him at breakfast in the morning. The men went to their jobs, all a bit happier than when they had collected an hour ago. On the way back to the kitchen, Kongolo texted James about Pressman seeing them pray for Victor. James read it and added it to his growing list of concerns. He headed back to his room to think and do some more praying. His heart was anxious from bearing so many different burdens.

Chapter 51

What James found when he returned to his room was an email response from the Israeli who wrote that dark web article that had so disturbed him. He was both excited and worried about what it would say.

```
Hello James,

My name is Aharon Biton. I am a
forty-two-year-old Israeli. I live
in Haifa. I am a communications
professor, though my specialty is
advanced encryption. I wrote the
article that you inquired about.
Please know that the information
provided is accurate. I believe
that this current Ebola outbreak is
being both monitored and manipulated
by very evil people. I would like
to talk more freely with you. Is
there a place where we could speak
without being overheard? Do you own
a disposable phone? Let me know when
and where works best for you.

Sincerely,
Aharon
```

James was devastated to learn that his suspicions were being confirmed. He wrote the man back, gave him the number to his burner phone, and made an appointment to speak with him at David's house around ten the next morning. He was all nerves as he pushed the send button. He immediately got confirmation back from the man, and the date and time were set.

James then texted David to say that he would be at his property to make a phone call, writing himself a note to follow up on those saddlebags while he was in town as well. James clicked his laptop closed and moved over to the wicker chair in the corner to think. He decided to look over his whole journal and all the coded notes that he had written for himself.

He finished the rest of Sunday in serious contemplation and had quiet meals with Lucas. James thought about Pressman's reaction to seeing Victor at the worship service. He climbed into bed with a heavy heart, realizing now there was no turning back. He laid awake for several hours and only fell asleep when he was finally able to truly turn everything back over to God.

Roosters everywhere, all crowing at once, woke him early the next morning. He was eager to get into the day, despite the lingering weight on his mind. If he wanted to finish his assignment, he would need to advance with precision. That meant being fully informed, so he looked forward to speaking with Aharon. He washed up, prepped for his day, and eagerly anticipated an early morning chat with Victor.

James entered the cafeteria, nodding to Kongolo in the kitchen, only to realize that Victor was not in his usual spot. For some reason, this rattled him a bit, but then he thought, *He's probably just running late.* James fixed his bread and coffee and downed two cups of water before sitting at his corner table.

He opened his journal and his Bible. Although he knew he could always read Scripture on his phone, he appreciated the comfort of physically holding the Book in his hands. And, because he had notes written throughout it, it was somehow like having a friend sitting with him when he felt almost abandoned. He turned to Psalm 27 again and read the whole thing through twice before intentionally focusing on each individual verse, deciding to make this his study for the duration of his stay in Congo.

> The LORD is my light and my salvation; whom shall
> I fear? The LORD is the strength of my life; of whom
> shall I be afraid?

James closed his eyes after reading the first verse, wanting to picture it in his mind, with all the punctuation. He wanted to be sure that it was etched there so that he could pull it up again without the aid of seeing it in print, just in case that light, salvation, and strength would be more specifically needed in the future.

Eating alone and wondering about Victor's continued absence, he went over to chat with Kongolo about Pressman's reaction to seeing the group pray for Victor, but Kongolo was not much help. Pressman had only glanced their way, and Kongolo had quickly averted his eyes so as not to be noticed, but he assured James it was not a positive expression.

The regular breakfast crowd filed in. Lucas sat down with his coffee and bread. He too was quiet, seemingly lost in thought. James leaned over. "Lucas, will you pray for me? I mean, like right now, out loud? I'm feeling really weighed down with everything that's going on. And, to add to that, Victor never showed up this morning. Would you pray for him, too? His family won't like the commitment he just made. I'm really afraid for him."

Lucas willingly jumped into prayer, interceding for James, the whole response team, and for Victor's protection. He prayed seeking God's will to be done which meant that evil would be defeated. He added that he hoped the victory would include the eradication of the disease. Further, he asked that his and James' families be granted comfort and strength in their tasks back at home. Finishing with an "amen," his emotion-strained voice showed his own anxiety. James thanked Lucas and the men parted ways to begin their day.

James was to have Paul pick him up at the front gate at 9:00 a.m. He postponed the weekly meeting with the security team for the next morning, wanting to pick up those saddlebags and have plenty of time to think before the phone call from Israel.

James found Paul quieter than usual. When he asked what was wrong, Paul remarked that he was worried about a cousin of his in Domiongo that was showing signs of the Ebola virus, and that his family was bringing him to the compound that morning for testing. James comforted him the best that he could but felt too burdened himself to be very encouraging. They rode in silence until they were parked outside the tailor's house.

Mama Odette had followed the directions for the saddlebags to the letter. James expressed his gratitude, paid the agreed price, then added a ten-dollar tip. Odette thanked him profusely as she watched him step back into the taxi. Two minutes later, they were pulling up to David's property on the south side of the town. David and his wife and children greeted him.

"Welcome, James. How are you doing today? Another special phone call, huh? Who is it this time?"

"A new contact, actually. Although, I might need to call Caleb after taking this phone call at ten, depending on what I find out. How are you and your family? Is everyone well?"

"Yes, thank you, Monsieur. We are all well. I assume that you will want privacy. I set up a chair by that mango tree over on the south side of my land. That way you will be able to speak freely. Can I have my daughter buy you a cold Coke? A friend down the street has just stocked his refrigerator."

"Thanks, David. That sounds great. If you don't mind, I'm going to go sit and write some things down before my call. I've still got twenty minutes, but I need to be sure I make note of everything that I want to ask so I don't forget anything."

James settled into his chair and waited for his Coke to arrive. At precisely ten a.m. the phone rang.

Chapter 52

"Hello, is this Aharon?"

"It is. Is this James?"

"Yes. So glad we could connect."

"I as well," Aharon replied. "I was surprised and pleased that you found my article and reached out. We all were."

This comment nearly caused James to drop the phone. "Wait. What? First of all, how do you know me, and who is we?"

"I cannot answer that at this time. And, you must know, you will continue to have questions, but I will not be able to give you the information you are looking for right away. That does not mean, however, that it is not coming. For now, the most important thing you need to know is that you are not alone."

"All right let's pretend for a moment that doesn't totally creep me out. How about we take a step back and just start at the beginning. Tell me a little more about yourself."

"As you already know, my name is Aharon Biton, I am forty-two years old and live in Haifa. I have a wife named Talia. We have been married for ten years, and we have two sons. I enjoy gardening and collecting heirloom seeds."

This comment seemed completely out of the blue to James, but he decided to simply file it away in his brain as Aharon continued.

"I am an advanced encryption expert. I studied this in university and teach it, but I have also been working in this field for the Israeli government for more than a decade. I am a Messianic Jew. I came to recognize Jesus as Messiah in my college years, I say this because I know that you, too, are a devoted Christ follower."

"How?" James interjected, trying not to sound as suspicious as he felt.

"I learned this by simply studying your social media profiles."

This put James slightly at ease, but he still wanted to keep his guard up.

"Now you may tell me about yourself, although I must say that I feel as if I already know you, sir."

"Well, I wish I could say the feeling was mutual, and I'm not exactly sure what I need to share. I'm afraid you have me at a little bit of a disadvantage here. I guess you already know that I am married to my high school friend, Julia. We also have two boys. We were reunited six years ago in Eastern Congo, where we were abducted by rebel forces. It was a harrowing experience, and we are thankful to have lived through it. I was a Special Forces soldier for eleven years with a focus in communications and, as you've probably read, I now teach it on a military base in Washington State. I'm one year from retiring, and I took this current assignment only under duress. The U.S. government explained that I was the perfect fit for it, yet here I am, quite frankly, scared out of my mind. My colleagues and I suspect the outbreak isn't being contained. So, when I read your article, it not only confirmed those fears, it amplified them." James hoped Aharon's response to that would bring him some sense of comfort, but that comfort never came.

"I want to assure you that the two primary claims I made in that article are true. The virus copyright is owned by the family I mentioned, and the lack of success of containing the outbreak is not by mistake. This sabotage has been planned."

"Okay?" James let out a breath, revealing his growing trepidation.

"But you must understand that not every evil organization in this world knows about this. Only a few, deeply connected players are involved."

"Are you trying to tell me it gets worse?" James poked.

"Sadly, yes. But when I say that you are not alone, I sincerely mean to strengthen you with the hope of your being able to succeed in your mission."

"Okay, Aharon," James started, "I know you're trying to encourage me, but the reality is that you have only managed to make me both more curious and more afraid. I'm not sure I can handle taking on the kind of giant forces involved in this situation."

"Surely you must be familiar with our famous David slaying Goliath."

James sighed as he realized his own hypocrisy in what he shared with the group of men less than twenty-four hours earlier. He was about to come clean when Aharon beat him to the punch and dropped a bombshell.

"Weren't you just studying this?"

"Okay, now how do you know that? Are you spying on me?" James pushed.

"Not spying. We are simply well-informed. But I must also say that the small miracle of Victor Archer coming to Christ will have a ripple-effect that could change the world someday. I cannot share everything with you now, but please know that I promise to warn you if I become aware of imminent danger. Apologies, but I need to cut this short. I first must stress, however, that the attack on the burial team is something to take very seriously. Please take extra precautions. Duty calls. I will contact you again soon."

With that, Aharon clicked off his phone, leaving James bewildered and visibly shaken. He sat there simply staring for several minutes, not reacting at all, just numb. Wanting to review the notes that he had taken, he decided to immediately translate them all into his personal code and destroy the originals by walking over to the family's cook fire and tossing them in.

Returning to his chair, James decided to call Caleb before leaving his solitude. Maybe talking over the phone with his friend would help him process things. He punched in Caleb's number. The phone rang several times but went to voicemail. He left a message asking Caleb to call him back if he got it within the next few minutes. He continued to sit in his chair and sip his Coke that David's daughter had brought while he was talking to Aharon. Staring out into the distance, James traced the road that led south out of Domiongo.

A lone Congolese trader was pushing a bicycle loaded high with sacks of manioc, also known as casava, heading to the market to trade the cash crop for other items like soap and salt. The man trudged along unaware of the turmoil swirling, not only in James' mind, but also in the whole region. For a moment, James felt a hint of jealousy toward the man's ignorance. How could he absorb the immensity of what he had just heard? But experience had taught him that he would likely get used to the weight of it all in the coming days, so he decided to take advantage of this time to just sit.

Allowing his mind to relax and wander for about fifteen minutes, he ultimately accepted that Caleb was not going to call. Having finished the Coke, he took a swig from his water bottle, gathered his things, and headed back to the house. He called Paul to let him know that he was ready to return to the compound.

James spent several minutes chatting with David's family and kicking a soccer ball with two of his sons, while waiting for his ride. As Paul pulled up, James thanked the family for their hospitality. They left for the compound, and James pondered the likelihood that this could be his last simple taxi ride for a long time. Lost in that thought, he was soon surprised to learn that they were already in front of the metal gates. James took his saddlebags, paid Paul, and waved goodbye to his once-ordinary life.

Chapter 53

James spent the rest of that day focused on the notes he took during his phone call with Aharon and studying his social media profile, which was very limited. He wanted to discuss the call with either Victor or Caleb, but Victor was still strangely absent, and Caleb was not responding to his messages.

As he looked things over, James paid close attention to those parts where Aharon hinted that he was not working alone. Who was the "we" that he referred to? Was it a committee or council? Were they an organized group with a specific agenda and mission, or were they simply a loose-knit group of like-minded colleagues? The mystery bothered him. And the fact that they thought that he was perfect for the tasks that lay before him also plagued his thoughts, as if he were chosen deliberately. Whoever it was, they sure seemed to know a lot about him.

James paused for a moment to consider that "chosen" part. He tried to think back to the day when Colonel Fitzwilliam called him. He had said that his name was brought up in a conversation about the response. *Who had the colonel been speaking to and what had been said,* he wondered. For now, though, he needed to concentrate on the tasks at hand. Friday was a planned burial for several patients who were expected to not survive the virus. Lucas had explained some of the issues, and James had already received warning about the complications of such a ceremony.

James decided to hold a meeting to gather volunteers to assist him in securing the burial team. Families in this region had certain customs that they followed when putting a loved one to rest, but the protocol for burying someone who had died of Ebola made some of those traditions impossible. In the past, families would show up in protest of the response teams' methods, but this time it sounded like it was likely to get violent. James called Facundo and his unit, Katey and his men, and asked Lucas and Kongolo to join him. He wished Victor would show up, but he had an odd feeling that he would not see him again, at least not on this mission.

James texted the men before supper, figuring four o'clock would give everyone who took a siesta a chance to be refreshed by that afternoon ritual. James hoped his mind would let him rest, knowing he needed it. But the combination of heat and stress would not allow him to relax, so he simply crawled out of the bed, wanting to have an hour before the meeting to organize his thoughts.

The men gathered in the empty cafeteria, mainly to concede to Kongolo's need to be near the kitchen. Kongolo was tasked again with sorting through beans for lunch the next day, a job he did throughout the meeting. The group discussed what had happened in the past with these burials and how they were to combat the potential escalation. James assigned Facundo and two of his men to join him, Katey, Kongolo, and Lucas to dig graves the day before the burial was to take place. They decided to eat an early breakfast and head out to the cemetery on Thursday to beat the heat. The group broke up with the gravity of the situation solid in their minds.

The cemetery was north of the village of Domiongo, but south of the compound. Katey had four men with him, who were all carrying ancient AK-47's. The guns may have been old, but they were packing plenty of ammunition. The two men that Facundo brought with him were also armed but had been instructed not to engage in combat. Their weapons were for self-defense only. James kept it simple. He had a sharpened knife hidden in his boot.

The group piled into a small taxi bus that Paul had borrowed for the occasion. Even with a larger vehicle, they barely fit. The original seats were long gone, probably being used as a sofa in someone's yard, and they had been replaced by thin benches. The day was already muggy, though the damp air still lingered from the night before. Katey sat up front with his brother. James was squished near the back of the vehicle. Being a little bit claustrophobic, he had already imagined needing to kick out that back window in case of an accident.

The bus turned onto a dirt path that was very grown over by the encroaching jungle. Soon, it opened up to what was a typical Congolese village cemetery. James had a difficult time even associating the place with that word. For one, it was not manicured at all. Secondly, almost all the gravesites were identifiable only by simple homemade markers, mostly crosses made of two pieces of wood tied together. The final thing that struck him was the lack of order since there seemed to be no straight lines anywhere. With sites spaced unevenly, the markers seemed to be propped up as headstones with no recognizable pattern.

The van pulled up and stopped in a section of the graveyard that was roped off by caution tape. This particular spot was reserved only for Ebola victims and had been purchased by the response from the city of Domiongo just for that purpose. The FARDC soldiers looked around skeptically as they tumbled out of the vehicle. James knew that Congolese were very wary of cemeteries. Many had heard stories about groups of people meeting in these places to collect themselves and teleport on spiritual airplanes, claiming to visit European capitals and dine well during the night, only to return in the morning full enough not to need a breakfast.

The men pulled shovels out of the van and took turns digging. The burial had been planned a few days prior, and since, three people had died of the virus. As of earlier that morning, two more deaths seemed imminent. At the rate people were losing their battles, the men decided to add an extra one to their itinerary, bringing the number of graves to six. The idea was to dig them ahead of time to limit the opportunity for rioting to occur in the morning. Their goal was to streamline the process of properly disposing of the corpses without spreading the virus.

Lucas directed the digging effort with initial instructions on how deep and far apart the graves should be and then lent his strength to the task. James, too, took his turn and was soon drenched to the skin with sweat. He pulled off his shirt, and the Congolese men did the same.

Within three hours, all six graves were complete. Each one was marked with a neon-painted stick, and then the men laid palm fronds over them to deter unwanted visitors.

Friday morning came way too early for everyone involved in the burial procedures, knowing the process had to be started before the sun was fully up. James and his crew met Lucas and several medical personnel at the clinic. Their task was only to observe, while those trained in the proper burial of an Ebola victim did the real work, following the detailed steps to dispose of the bodies. Lucas and his team were fully covered in their PPE suits.

Each of the five corpses, already wrapped in three separate body bags which were properly sealed and sanitized, was lying on sterilized mortuary stretchers. Each bag was labeled with four different tags: a black and white one that read "infectious substance," one that said "UN 2814," another that simply stated, "do not open," and a fourth with the name and phone number of the hospital administrator.

Several taxi buses had to be hired that were large enough to accomodate one or two body bags apiece. Each vehicle had been sterilized by trained clinic staff. The bodies were loaded in by men wearing protective gear, and the doors were shut. Those with Katey were to lead the entourage. James, Kongolo, Facundo and his men, who rode in a vehicle at the end of the line of taxi buses. No one was sure what would meet them at the cemetery. The nerves of everyone in that last vehicle were taut.

No sooner were all the taxis out of the compound gate than the trouble began.

Chapter 54

The men knew that they were in trouble. Crowds of angry villagers lined the road on either side, most of them friends of the Ebola victims. Almost everyone knows that a mob as large as the one they were facing was, even in the best circumstances, volatile, deadly in extreme cases, but in the Congo, funeral mobs were the worst. The local soldiers grabbed their weapons tighter out of sheer instinct.

Katey's taxi was forced to slow down as men swarmed the path. All the cars screeched to a halt, making them extremely vulnerable. As soon as the convoy stopped, the vehicles were overtaken. The rioters were climbing on the roofs of each car, kicking and beating on the windows. James immediately called Katey and demanded that he drive forward, even if it was slowly, needing to put the crowd behind them as soon as possible.

Katey agreed and got everyone moving again. Soon they reached the turnoff toward the cemetery. Although many protestors jumped off as the vehicles picked up speed, each taxi still had one or two on top.

James had one of them sprawled across the windshield of his car. "Get off!" he growled, angry that this already complex task had gotten so out of control. "Tika. Bozonga na ndako na yo! Go home!" He continued repeating his commands, but the young man persisted, sticking his fist through the open passenger window and attempting to grab James by the shirt front. James, much stronger and quicker, yanked the man off the hood of the car by his arm and threw him forcefully on the ground with a thud. Since their car was moving fast enough, the man couldn't get himself upright in time to reattack the vehicle. Soon, most of the mob was left at the main road and the entourage was fast approaching the entrance to the cemetery which appeared to have no waiting crowd.

The vehicles pulled up to the far side of the area where the graves had been dug the day before. Dismay greeted them like an unwanted guest as they found that all the graves had been filled in during the night, making their chances of being hindered by onlookers grow exponentially.

James stumbled out in utter disbelief, followed by Katey and his men. Shovels appeared, as men handed them out of the vehicles, and everyone began frantically re-digging the graves. Although they were frustrated by the process of having to redo everything they had just done hours before, the fact that the dirt was loose made the job move faster. Just as the first corpse was about to be lowered into the ground, a group of hostiles emerged from the forest surrounding the cemetery. They first made their presence known by throwing rocks, then made their demands.

"Tika ete tolonga bizalaleli na biso!"

Stones pelted the Congolese personnel who were lowering the remains. They dodged the projectiles as best as they could, but it was obvious that the annoyance would slow their progress. "They are insisting we let them follow their own customs," Kongolo shouted as he, James, and Katey stepped between what they assumed were angry family members and the men doing the labor.

James ordered everyone to turn their backs on the crowd to avoid being hit in the face but positioned himself to keep an eye on what appeared as a no-win situation. He then walked closer to the one who was obviously the leader of the group. The man was in his late twenties, intelligence shone from his clear eyes. "Mpo na nini ozali kosala likambo oyo?" James questioned, demanding an answer for why they were doing this.

For a split second, the man glanced behind him into the jungle, almost as if he were awaiting instructions. James followed his look and was shocked to see that his gaze ended at someone crouched down, poking his head out, just behind a tree a short distance into the foliage, but close enough that James could immediately spot a pronounced cleft in his chin.

"What are you doing here? Who are you?"

No sooner had the man been spotted than he bolted south through the jungle. James began a chase that, based on his previous experience, he was most likely not going to be able to finish. The man continued on a path that was obviously very familiar to him, leaving James bumbling along, attempting to find it.

Katey had noticed the chase and had stepped into James' position of being between the rioters and the burial team. But it was no longer necessary. As soon as they knew that the mundele leader had been discovered, they were so distracted that they stopped their protest to watch the chase. Lucas and the others, seeing their opportunity, rushed to finish their task while they had the chance.

James was huffing and puffing as he caught the trail and picked up his pace with the pursuit leading all the way to an old part of town that was built by the Belgians prior to 1960. He really hoped he would apprehend the man this time, but then he turned down a side street where there were walled houses and, once again, the man was nowhere to be seen. No sound of a gate closing could give him any clue as to which house the man had disappeared into. He hated to admit defeat, but James decided to return to the cemetery to question the protestors.

Back at the gravesites, James found a completely different scene than the one he had fled. Everyone was eerily calm. Katey was questioning the crowd, not in French or Lingala, but in a more local tongue, Kindengese. After a few minutes, Katey finally turned toward James. "This man is confessing for the whole group that this entire protest was planned and paid for by the man that you just chased. Any idea who that was?"

"Sort of," James started, "I think it's the guy I've been talking about. The one I caught spying on me. I don't know who he is though. I've never been close enough to get a good look at him. I can't say anymore in front of the group. Can you ask them what they can tell us about this guy?"

Katey translated once again in Kindengese. Several began speaking at once and pointing to their chins, but one young man was pointing to his eyes. Katey turned back toward James. "They all noticed the mark on his chin. But this young man said that his eyes are also unusual. His left one is blue, but the right one is a dark brown."

James stopped and recalled all that Aharon had said about this response, especially about it being intentionally sabotaged. He once again felt that all-too-familiar mounting sense of dread. Breathing out slowly, trying to manufacture mental peace, James thanked Katey for questioning the group and asked him to instruct them to refrain from reporting back to the man that they had confessed what they knew. Katey agreed and sent the men home with a vow to place the security of their village above the desire for a payoff.

James turned back to the whole burial team. Some were simply staring at him, looking for direction or meaning, but all were physically exhausted and hungry. "Let's get back to the compound, clean up, and grab our late breakfast. We have to keep quiet about what happened here today. If we all swear to silence, but then we hear about it on the compound, it may be easier to ascertain where it's coming from. Are we all in agreement on this?" Everyone nodded their heads quietly, still sobered by the morning's events.

Chapter 55

James heard no talk of the burial encounter all the rest of that Friday. On Saturday morning, he rose early as usual. He really missed his chats with Victor. Wondering where he was, he decided to text him on both cell numbers that he had. He didn't expect a response, but he got one.

> Hello, James. I am glad you reached out. I'm well, but as you can guess, my family was not all that excited about my decision to follow Christ. They abruptly called me home. Since they knew of it so quickly, I assume that there is still an enemy in the compound. Be constantly vigilant. If I learn anything specific, I will text you a warning. Please be careful.

James thanked him for his friendship and warning. Without Victor on the grounds, he felt less confident, but he liked the idea that a well-connected man had his back, even from a distance.

James had breakfast with Lucas, who was mostly quiet. Both men were deeply worried about their own safety and that of the response team. The fact that the previous day's attack had been planned from an outside source drove home the thought that this crisis was larger than their capacities to manage it. Neither had that level of experience in their backgrounds, either medical or military. He knew that they both faced the challenge of being a whistle-blower, an unenviable task, with the subject frequently being criticized from all sides.

James decided to bring it up. "Lucas, just to prepare you to start thinking of a plan, we might be called upon at some point to share the unusual events of this international response. Whistleblowers are rarely treated with respect but testifying might be our reality at some point. Please think through anything you might want to share and have a strategy in place to shield your family from the fall out."

"James, I just can't believe the level of evil that is involved in this outbreak. What happened yesterday, the dead lesula, and some of the things you shared are beyond our expertise. I know we need to be prepared to do the right thing, but I don't know if I'm brave enough."

"I understand."

"I became a doctor so that I could save lives. I just never thought that it would ever require me to save my own. This unseen enemy is deadlier than the disease." Lucas shuddered at the thought.

With nothing more to say, the men finished breakfast in silence.

Since it was a Saturday, James did not have any official business to do. He decided to once again review his notes from the phone call with Aharon. He said goodbye to Lucas and headed back to his room. He took a quick run to the bathroom first and was shocked to round the corner and nearly run into Pressman who, interestingly enough, seemed to have been waiting for him.

"James, I wanted to have a word with you. Do you have a minute?"

"Sure. What's on your mind?"

"I think you're taking your role here too seriously. I believe that it is time to step back a bit from the passion you seem to bring to your job. No one appreciates an over-achiever."

James was incredulous. "Are you really saying that I don't need to work hard to protect the people on this compound?"

"Of course not. You need to do your job. No one wants the response to be vulnerable or weak. What I'm speaking about is being over-zealous, making secret trips to the village, handling riots and protests by yourself. No one is expecting you to be a hero here. You need to report everything to me. Am I clear?"

James had a few snappy retorts come to mind but refrained from sharing them, since it was obvious that Pressman had been spying on him. He wondered how he had found out about the second riot and the trips to town. He decided to reroute the conversation. "Do you happen to know where Victor is? He had worship with us Sunday, and we have not seen him since then. Did something happen? Was he called home on an emergency?"

Pressman turned red, then gray; his eyes hardened and brows furrowed. Regaining his composure, he made a statement which James knew to be untrue. "His paper called him back to London to work on another, more delicate piece. He won't be back to report on this outbreak."

James nodded his head in assent, said goodbye, and finished his business before heading back to his chamber. On his way, he received a text from Kongolo asking him what Pressman had to say. James laughed out loud. The guy thought he was being secretive and threatening, but he was no match for the sharp eyes of the Congolese.

James waited until he was inside before texting back, then opened his laptop to study Google Earth. Before he could even put in the region of Congo that he wanted to view, he got a text from Caleb asking if it was a good time to talk. James jumped at the chance to share the recent events and his conversation with Aharon. He anxiously dialed Caleb's number.

Chapter 56

"Hey, James. How are you? I've been worried about you, man. I've half a mind to jump on a plane and come help you battle the forces of evil." Caleb finished with a chuckle, being purposefully overdramatic, but was taken aback by James' response.

"Brother, you have no idea how accurate that last phrase is. If I told you everything, you'd have a whole Special Forces unit here within twenty-four hours."

"Wow, really? I didn't know it had gotten so serious."

James went on. "I really need to bounce some things off you. Do you have about fifteen minutes to spare? I can hardly wrap my mind around all I haven't told you yet. And now that I know my room is clean, I feel freer to talk here. Just can't be too loud."

"Wait, was your room bugged?" Caleb questioned.

"Yup."

"How did you figure that out? Do you know who was listening on the other end? Actually, just start from the last time we talked."

James told him about all he had learned from Victor concerning the global conspiracy surrounding the depopulation goals of certain people. Reviewing the confrontation with J.P. and the conversation Kongolo had overheard about her being purposefully sent to sabotage him, he then informed him of her disappearance, as well as Victor's. He continued with the rioting at the burial, the attack, and how the young men had claimed to have been paid to stage it. James finally got to the thing he was most anxious to discuss.

"But what I really want to share in detail is the conversation with this Israeli that I met through an article site on the dark web. His name is Aharon Biton. He says he's a cryptologist."

"I'm listening," Caleb encouraged.

"He wrote an article claiming that this medical response is intentionally being thwarted to see how much the disease would spread if certain protocols were not precisely followed. He also said that the Ebola virus actually is patented and owned by a single family, whose name you can probably guess. He finished by saying that I was perfect for the task of combating this evil. He knew a lot about me, not just things easily found on social media. He finished by promising me that he and his group had my back, and that he would warn me about specific or imminent threats."

Caleb gave a low whistle.

James asked, "What do you think of all this?"

"Well, it's a lot."

"Does it sound plausible to you, though? I'm half hoping that he's just a nut, but with all that I've seen, I'm inclined to believe him."

"Yeah. He sounds like he'd be credible. If I were in your shoes, I would lean toward believing him. That would be the safest thing to do at this point. So, what can I do for you on this side? I can gain approval to have a team on standby to jump in and assist you if it comes to that."

"Thanks, Caleb. It actually would give me peace of mind to know that I had backup ready to help if needed. Do you really think that you can get the go ahead to do that?"

"Positive," Caleb confirmed.

"Go through Fitzpatrick just to be sure that we won't be stepping on any international or political toes with this. Hey, I gotta go. Please text me every few days to see if I'm okay. I'd appreciate that."

"Sure. I'll keep in touch. I'll start working on that team. You're not alone. Aharon is right. You can do this. No one is better equipped to take down this giant of an evil than you. Love you, bro. I'll be praying for you."

The men said their goodbyes, and James ended the call feeling a little more encouraged than he had ten minutes earlier.

Chapter 57

James woke on Sunday thinking how hard it was to believe that it had only been a week since their last worship time. One was planned again for that morning at nine, but of course, Victor would not be there to enjoy the fellowship. He took a few minutes to pray for Victor's safety and that his faith would not waiver no matter what challenges he faced.

Before heading into his day, he decided to call Julia. It would be Saturday afternoon there, a good time. He dialed her number.

"Good morning, Julia, or rather good afternoon. How are you doing, Babe? Hanging in there?"

"Yeah. I'm good. Just missing you. So are the boys. They ask constantly when you'll be home. Being a single parent is not for the faint of heart, that's for sure. How's it going there? Any easier? I've been praying for you."

"I appreciate that. You have no idea how much that means to me." James paused to clear his throat. "Jules, I'm calling really with just a short caution. I want you to mentally and emotionally prepare yourself for some scary news. I've discovered that I have very powerful enemies here. Spiritual wickedness in high places, literally. You might get word that I've gone missing or rogue. Don't believe anything you hear from anyone except me, Caleb, or Fitzpatrick. Okay? I need you to promise me this."

"Of course, James. But you're really freaking me out. Are you in over your head? Should I contact anyone here about this?"

"No. No need. Caleb is taking care of things on that side. He'll prepare to jump in if I need help. Just be patient. Sit tight. Love those boys for me. I promise to connect with you every day, at least by text. If a day goes by without hearing from me, you'll know that circumstances are getting crazy. Understand?"

"Yes." Julia paused a moment before continuing, "I'm terrified that I'll never see you again. Please keep checking behind you. Make sure that no one is going to catch you off guard. I love you."

"I love you, too. Bye, Babe."

James stood up but the weight of everything caused him to just sit right back down again. He dropped his head into his hands and stared at the floor, rocking back and forth in his chair in an attempt to quiet the evil thoughts crowding his mind. He remained in this position for a while, not even in control enough to pray through his despair. He knew that he had just placed terror into Julia's heart, and it grieved him, making him lack the strength to move forward into his day.

Finally, he stood up again and grabbed his shower caddie. The freezing water did more to revive him than he could have thought. Back in the room, he grabbed his Bible, journal, and notes on his phone call from Aharon. He wanted to evaluate them side-by-side with his Bible study, needing his fears to be as close as possible to the strength and wisdom of the Word.

Settling himself into his corner in the cafeteria, surrounded by his favorite things: coffee, bread, Scripture, his journal, and music, he started his Sunday with a worship song, and then decided to read the last few verses of Isaiah forty, a place he could depend upon to gain strength. Though he started with verse twenty-eight, he focused on twenty-nine to thirty-one.

> He gives power to the faint; and to them that have no might He increases strength. Even the youths shall faint and be weary, and the young men shall utterly fall: But they that wait upon the LORD shall renew their strength; they shall mount up with wings as eagles; they shall run, and not be weary; they shall walk, and not faint.

James felt deep within him the fatigue, weariness, and weakness of the young man in the passage. He openly acknowledged that he was not strong enough or smart enough to combat the enemy in this place. As the walls began closing in and the possibility of needing to flee was becoming more of a reality, he knew that he would need minute-by-minute, detailed help from God Himself, not only to survive, but also to complete his mission of keeping the response team and the village safe. He'd need wisdom to do both.

He took several minutes to review the verses repeatedly, taking notes on the waiting part and wondering if there was a practical application. He finished his coffee and bread, went back for seconds, and then was joined by Kongolo from the kitchen and Lucas from the courtyard. They sat down for a few minutes with James and prayed.

James discussed with Lucas the implication of Isaiah 40:31. "Do you think waiting on the LORD is a practical strategy, Lucas? Can it be relied upon in a crisis to meet a need for strength or wisdom or direction?"

"Hmm, never thought of it as practical, more just spiritual or emotional. But you might be onto something there. If God can direct you better spiritually if you slow down and wait for Him, why couldn't He help if you literally slow down and move only under His direction? Seems like something that I need to practice here in the clinic. We're both under extreme stress right now."

"Truth. We should explore this passage more closely at worship this morning. Are you going to be there?"

"Yup. I'm finished here and need to check on some patients, but

I'll be there at nine."

Lucas left the table and James sat still, quietly pondering the verse.

The group met in the common room as planned. It was convenient for Kongolo to worship there with everyone since he worked every day on the compound. Although he was a member at a small congregation in town, as was Katey, he hadn't been able to make it there on Sundays since the start of the outbreak. Just getting out of kitchen duty was a tough call, but his boss did not want to disappoint James, nor stand in the way of any security that could only be enhanced by the blessings of God. As Facundo was passing the door, he looked in and asked to join the men as well.

Now that the group was complete, the service began. After singing two songs, the men delved into Isaiah forty. James brought up the potential for verse thirty-one being practical as well as emotional or spiritual. Everyone had some thoughts to add, but Kongolo gave his interpretation by telling his perspective of James and Julia being kidnapped as an illustration.

He reiterated the details he'd told them the previous week, adding in a few more new ones for clarity and context. Kongolo once again affirmed that James and Julia's abduction, although horrific, was a direct answer to his sister's prayers.

"I see us in these verses. Dinanga and I were young but were without strength. We were so terrified that we were too faint to try to escape on our own. But we waited. God sent us this man to strengthen us to run. Not only were my sister and I saved, but the whole encampment of women and children were freed. I thank God for His promise here, for James and Julia. Their hardship became our chance for a new life."

James' eyes were wet with unshed tears. Lucas gave him a pat on the back. "Kongolo, thank you for sharing this, but I must confess that with this mission, I am now the weak and faint youth. I will need all your help, prayers, and encouragement to do what's required to keep this compound and response safe. Please pray for me now. Lucas, would you start?"

Each man present took turns praying for James, who was obviously scared, and poured out their souls. James' success would be theirs; his safety would be their safety. They knew this.

When the group was finished, they broke up and returned to their duties for the day. James prepared himself to head into his fifth week in Congo. It seemed as if he had been there for years. A sigh escaped his lips as he walked back to his room, trying to mentally prepare himself for the numerous possibilities that could lay ahead.

The next morning, James decided to use the time between breakfast and the security meeting to again review Aharon's phone call. Wanting to be sure that he was missing nothing vital, he got out his notes and read them all through twice, then decided to go through a third time with a pencil and make notes along the sides to help him focus his thinking.

The first thing he marked was that the sabotage of the virus response was planned and not accidental. He then listed questions about this based on what he knew.

```
1. Was the plan to do this for the
whole length of the outbreak?
2. Was it for part of the outbreak,
just long enough to do experiments
and collect data?
3. Was the dead lesula a part of
that plan to undermine the success
of the mission to stamp out the
disease in this area?
4. If yes, who was conducting that
experiment and where did they do
it without being noticed by other
members of the clinical staff?
5. What about J.P.'s role? Was she
really sent to slow me down or stop
me completely?
```

James shuddered at the thought of how his succumbing to her strategy would have ruined everything in his life that he held dear, not to mention how this all affected the world at large. He shook his head again, feeling the weight of the position he was in. He closed his eyes, rubbed his temples, and continued his list.

```
6. Aharon had hinted that he knew
just where he had been studying in
Scripture. How would he know such an
intimate detail?
```

```
7. Was the whole compound under
surveillance?
```

James stopped a minute to think back about whether or not he had used his phone to study that passage, recalling that he had looked up a word in the online version of Strong's Concordance.

```
8. Did Aharon have access to his
phone?
9. If yes, was everyone under such
close scrutiny or was it just him
because of his position?
```

After making his list of questions, the point he focused on the most was what Aharon had said about his safety, his family's safety, and the success of the mission to stop the spread of the disease. James wondered how one man in a far distant country was so certain of such assurances. This final thought, however, gave James more courage than he had felt in weeks. Knowing that someone out there somewhere was on his side instilled great comfort. He knew that he could count on God to help him, but God very often used human means to complete His goals.

Finishing his notes, he trotted over to start the security staff meeting which was being held in the cafeteria so that the men could enjoy bread and drinks more easily. It went off without a hitch. Facundo purposefully did not bring up the riot before the other men. But afterwards, he discussed it in detail with James. He talked over the idea of someone actually paying the locals to put on this protest at the burial, and how they should proceed with that information.

"Sir, I am quite worried about this. If my commander in Kinshasa knew of this, he would pull us all off this mission. We are here only as an extra layer of security. If he knew that we were intentionally ambushed, he would be very upset. What should I do?"

"For now, don't say anything to your commander. I need you here as an additional set of eyes and ears. You now know what I am dealing with, and I do not wish to do this without the support of you and your men. Just hold off reporting this for a few days. I promise to let you know if you should explain things to him. I do not want you in danger, but I also need your attention to detail right now."

"All right, sir. I understand. I will keep this unreported until you say otherwise. Thank you for how thorough you are being. I am in your debt, and so are my men." With that Facundo excused himself to go about his typical duties.

On Tuesday morning, just as he was walking away from the shower building, James got a text on his cheap phone from an Israeli country code number. It inquired as to whether there was a safe place to chat. James asked for three minutes to get himself in a secure location. After dropping his shower tote and towel in his room, he took a walk down the path to the clinic. Between it and the living area was a place about as private as James could find. No one from either location could easily overhear the conversation. He took a deep breath and sent a final text.

314   I'm ready.

Chapter 58

James answered his phone before the first ring was done.

"Hello, James," Aharon greeted. "How are you this morning?"

"I'm well, thanks, despite all that's going on."

"Good. I hope you are sleeping well and eating properly. It's imperative that you stay in good health, or at least the best that you can."

"I'm managing," James conceded. "I have to admit that it's actually easier to stay physically healthy than it is to stay mentally strong. There have been some rather significant events that have occurred that we need to discuss. I'm not sure how you are getting your intelligence about what is going on here. Were you informed about the rioting and attack on the burial team?" James prepared to write down notes as he turned on the voice recorder of his cell phone.

"I am not aware of this. Tell me about it and don't leave anything out."

"We believe the attack was not just planned by locals; it was orchestrated by outside forces. We had heard ahead of time that occasionally there are issues with the burials of Ebola victims. The family members have customs that are typically broken by following the safety protocols of the medical response team. These families have been known to show up at the site to throw rocks at those performing the burials, usually members of the clinic staff."

"Okay," Aharon said.

"To prevent as much of a problem as possible, we dug the graves the day before."

"Good planning."

"On Friday morning," James continued, "as we were leaving the compound, our vehicles were slowed down by protestors along the road and then attacked. Young men were climbing all over the slowed cars and vans, and others were throwing rocks and chunks of cement at the vehicles."

"Were you able to move past them without injuring any of the protestors? It is very important for you to stay in the good graces of those from that village."

"Yes. We were able to move past the protestors, turn off the main road, and then reach the cemetery without further incident. But that wasn't the end of our problems. At the burial site, we realized that the graves had been filled in by locals during the night. That was a surprise to me because the population is normally very superstitious about entering the graveyard after dark. Once we were out of our vehicles, we saw that more rioters were approaching from the surrounding forest. They began to throw rocks at the men who were attempting to re-dig the graves, slowing down their progress. I finally had enough. I stepped between the protestors and the clinic workers to block them, when I saw, deep into the forest, someone I recognized."

"Who was it?" Aharon fired off rapidly.

"I'm not sure of his exact identity, but I'm positive I've personally seen this man at least three times that I can recall. Twice, I had caught someone peering into my window in the middle of the night. The first time, he ran away as soon as he knew I had noticed him, but the second time, I chased him. I was only able to see a deep cleft in his chin but caught no other features. Then, a young man at the clinic claimed he was bribed by someone to not perform all his sanitizing duties, breaking protocol. He spoke of the cleft, so I knew it had to be the same person. Finally, my Congolese friend Kongolo overheard someone speaking to two members of the western response team that I suspect are complicit in this attempted sabotage. He reported back to me that the man had a cleft chin, as well as one blue eye and one brown eye. So, when the protestors at the gravesite later confessed to seeing this same man and explicitly mentioned he had two different colored eyes, it was confirmed that all those events had involved the same person, and he is definitely not on our side."

"Who are these westerners that have you so worried? I probably should follow up on my end to be sure that they have no real aim of harming you personally."

"I appreciate that, Aharon. One is a female reporter, who has since disappeared rather mysteriously. Her name is J.P. Walker. Victor, who is no longer here either, by the way, warned me of her. Kongolo had specifically overheard the group I mentioned explaining the fact that J.P. was only here to seduce me, thereby ruining my reputation and my capacity to do my duties to secure this mission."

"I can see how that would be very upsetting to a man of your integrity."

"It was. Still is, actually. Even though she's gone." James let out a sigh and then continued, "Anyway, the other westerner seems to be highly placed but less powerful. His name is Jim Pressman. He's a Brit who oversees the general operations of the compound."

"I understand. So, return to your story about this man at the burial attack. Did you pursue him?"

"I did, but I lost him somewhere in those walled, old Belgian houses on the northeast side of Domiongo. When I returned to the cemetery, several of the young rioters claimed that they had been promised money from him if they showed up to protest the burial. It was then that I reminded them about the seriousness of this disease. I made them all promise to tell no one about the guy. I wanted to be able to follow up on him without alerting the whole village."

"Okay, James. I have a good picture of what you are up against. I want you to spend the next few days specifically preparing to extricate yourself, should that become necessary. Browse the internet for old routes that you could take away from the region. Pack a go-bag for flight and any weapons that could help you. I promise that if I hear of anything specific that I will text you a warning. Do you have any resources or connections that you've made that would benefit you in this scenario?"

"I've brought in a trusted friend who's back in the states, Caleb Baker. He's working on this as we speak. We've been communicating through what I believe to be secure means. He has the ability to bring people in to continue the mission should I need to leave. I appreciate knowing that, if I do have to go, there are people I trust who can come in and finish the job. I do love the Congolese people and my friends here. Knowing that they would be taken care of eases my mind."

"Well, take further comfort in the fact that are very good and powerful people you don't know who are also on your side and prepared to help you if needed. They want to see this virus eradicated, not only in Congo but around the globe."

"Thank you, Aharon. Just try to give me as much advance notice as possible if I need to get out of here."

"I promise, James. Goodbye for now. I hope sometime that we

can sit down in a safe place and enjoy getting to know each other better over a cup of coffee. Until then, take care of yourself."

With that, Aharon hung up and left James to sort out his new information. He wrote notes in his code and memorized the recording of the call before deleting it from his phone.

Chapter 59

James spent the rest of that day reviewing his notes from the phone call, simultaneously creating additional notes from them for a call with Caleb sometime later that week. With that finished, he began brainstorming ways he could flee quickly, should that need arise. His mind immediately went to the Indian. He decided to heed Aharon's advice and look up old routes in that region of the Congo. Not sure where to begin, he typed in *motorcycle*, *Congo*, and *Africa* into his search bar. He scrolled down several pages until he found some unique information.

The Cairo to Capetown motorcycle race from the early 1900's caught his attention. James had never heard of such a thing. Apparently, a century of conflict on the African continent had halted this amazing challenge, but a renewed interest was obvious by the amount of tour packages that popped up. Once he opened the page, he realized there was a language barrier as most of the information was in French and German. Knowing that it would take too much time to use Google translate to interpret such a high volume of words, he started trying to streamline the process by skimming through the articles looking for sentences specifically involving Belgian Congo, Leopoldville, and Port Franqui.

He soon found himself delving into articles about outdated road conditions; interesting, but not what he needed. He was finally reduced to using Google Earth to study the roads in the area, which he couldn't be sure was completely up to date, but at least more current than the most recent article he could find. Making some notes, he drew himself a primitive map on some graph paper. He used the atlas app to create a simple escape route, but he decided to ask Katey and Kongolo about road conditions and older paths. He figured he needed less well-known ones if he was going to be able to outsmart an enemy.

The next morning, James showed Kongolo and Katey his drawing and asked for clarification about alternative routes out of the area, both north and south, setting off some mental alarm bells.

"James," Katey said, "what do you know that we don't? Why are you planning a way to leave your post? Won't you get in trouble for that?"

"Yeah, I'm worried about that, too. But I have information that scares me enough that I would rather err on the side of caution and have a plan in place that I hope I will never have to use, than risk being caught in the crossfire."

At this, both men clucked their tongues, a typical Congolese response.

"But what about us?" Katey interjected with honest, personal concern. "How would we be kept safe if you were gone? Our whole region could be impacted by the Ebola virus. Our wives and children could die."

"I've been assured that the response and you all would be protected if I were forced to escape a situation where I was the specific target. I'm sure that everything will be okay for all of you. I'm needing to trust my source, and I'm asking you to trust me. Can you both do that?"

The men nodded their heads and agreed to James' request for confidentiality on this subject.

On Friday morning, after breakfast, James took the time to create an escape to-do list and load his saddle bags with necessities. He packed the knife that Kongolo had provided. Thankful for it, he spent a few minutes making sure it was as sharp as possible. James added in food and water, maps, notebooks, external phone chargers, two flashlights that he had bought in the village, extra batteries, medical supplies, and a change of clothes. Then he prepared all his legal documents and placed them in a waterproof bag. He had found a windbreaker being sold by a used clothes vendor, with a Joe's Plumbing logo on the front. Somehow that logo made him laugh, something he had not done much of since he had been in Congo. Once the bags were packed, he practiced tying them down on the motorcycle.

Just then, it occurred to him that he would need extra fuel and oil, and he made a mental note on his way back to the compound to ask Kongolo to purchase several liters. Once he had those supplies safely stored, he breathed a bit easier. Knowing that he could escape at a moment's notice was good for his peace of mind.

James finished the preparations with texts to both Caleb and Julia. He told Caleb, rather cryptically, to have a team on standby. He told Julia that he was confident he was as ready as he could be for any contingency, wanting her to have a sense of security. Her response was positive but obviously subdued.

Kongolo showed up for work and tapped on James' door. He didn't step in, but he promised James that if he needed to flee that he would ride with him as far as the river. This gave James a good deal of comfort, and he accepted the offer of company. He just hoped that Kongolo would already be on the compound if such an act became necessary. In the end, they decided on a rendezvous point on the north side of Domiongo, if the possibility became a reality. The men parted, once again finding themselves united in a fight for their lives.

Chapter 60

Saturday brought with it a false sense of calm and muggy simplicity. Early July in Congo was right in the middle of the long, dry season, and often the days began foggy. This usually burned off by mid-morning, replacing the brief coolness with an intense, blazing heat.

James was up looking around his room, taking a mental inventory of irreplaceable objects and additional things that could fit into the saddlebags or his emergency backpack. His ruck sack would have to stay behind, but he decided he needed to take his Bible, his laptop and other electronic devices, and his family pictures. Clothes could be replaced. Other things, like food and water, could be purchased at small village markets as he travelled. He knew he needed Congo francs for giving "gifts" along the way. Fleeing would need stealth and secrecy, which could be bought. He didn't want the inability to bribe himself out of a mess to be an obstruction to his progress. Thankfully, he already had one hundred dollars worth of francs, and he also had two hundred dollars in a combination of American tens and twenties.

After lunch, he read his Bible, journaled, listened to calming music, and prayed more earnestly than ever before. He focused most of his attention on the request for wisdom and revisited that "wait on the LORD" passage from Isaiah, contemplating once again whether that could really be used as a survival strategy. With that weighing on his mind, he went to supper.

As James was getting ready to go to bed that night, a text came through from Aharon asking for a quick call. Before he could type a response, another one came through from Victor telling him that he needed to get away from the compound. Despite his surprise at once again hearing from his friend, and his strong desire to ask a myriad of questions, James knew he didn't have time for that. He just texted Victor back a quick "thank you" and then nervously told Aharon to call him.

The phone rang almost immediately. Just as quickly, James picked up. Before he could say anything, Aharon shouted from the other end, "James, you need to get out of there. Are you ready?"

"I guess I have to be. What exactly is going on?"

"I believe," Aharon continued, "that there is a team on their way to the village with the specific mission of eliminating you. You'll have about an eight-hour head start if you leave immediately. Alert your contact from the states but know that we will also be sending a team to assist you. They will be on the ground about the same time as the enemy which could put you in the middle of a warzone. For the teams to be where you are with precision, you will need to text me updates as to your location and travel times."

Stunned and still processing everything, all James could utter was, "Okay."

"Your safety is our priority," Aharon continued. "If men are fighting behind you, keep moving. You need to get to the river. Once on your way, head for the city of Ilebo. Someone will meet you there at the port. Take care, my friend, and go with God!"

James clicked off the phone and immediately called Kongolo who was still on the property, having just finished cleaning up the kitchen for the night. James explained what he had just learned and told him to wait outside the front gate. He then called Katey and informed him that the warning had come through, tasking him with the job of collaborating with the village chief to find the mysterious man who had been orchestrating these events. Katey promised that he would and wished for God to give James speed and safety. The final call was to Caleb, giving him the green light.

James went to the bathroom, packed up his backpack, adjusted the saddlebags one last time, and quietly pushed the Indian to the front gate. Once there, he simply nodded to the sentinel, who asked no questions. Outside the gate, Kongolo was waiting and took a turn pushing the motorcycle north on the dirt road until they were far enough away from the compound. Without a word, James started the bike and Kongolo hopped onto the back.

Once they were far from civilization, James explained to Kongolo about the eight-hour head start, the mercenary soldiers, and the two teams moving in to assist. Kongolo asked some questions, wanting to know specifics about the warnings from Aharon and the proposed route.

As they approached a split in the road, James asked which way they needed to go to get to the river. "I have been instructed to find a boat to take me to Ilebo," he added as his heart raced.

"Au gauche."

Understanding enough French to know what this meant, James turned left as Kongolo continued. "It is a more direct path, but the river will still be at least six hours away. Plus, we will need to stop for gas, adding even more time. It is going to be a long journey. If you need me to take over the driving, I can, provided you show me how."

"Thanks, Kongolo," James replied, appreciating his friend's sentiments but nowhere near comforted.

As they continued to travel, James' mind drifted to the tasks he both had and had not completed on the compound. While he was thankful that he had taken the time to fix up the motorcycle he was now using to escape, he couldn't help but feel a little regret over not taking the time to investigate the tunnel under the trapdoor in the same depot he had found that bike. Little did James know, however, he would have further opportunity in the future.

About an hour out of Domiongo, they came to a small village. A few campfires were still burning. James bought some kwanga for Kongolo to snack on. The sour, fermented manioc dough was not his thing, but he did get some peanuts for himself, which he wolfed down. Both men drank plenty of water. Kongolo took his turn on the bike as the two men fled north into the night.

Caleb texted James several times while they were on the road, attempting to pinpoint his exact location. He and a group of six men were in-route on a private flight from Morocco to Kananga. There they were to obtain a helicopter to drop them as close to James as possible. With him was one former Congolese soldier who had been training in the States, and a member of the French national strike team. Try as he might to find out about this force coming against James, he just couldn't seem to make all the right connections. He asked James for additional information who, in turn, texted to ask Aharon. Aharon got back pretty quickly, knowing how important it was to James and the two teams heading there to defend him.

> The team that has the assignment
> to eliminate you is from South
> Africa. It is not a government-
> approved team, but rather a small

unit from a mercenary company
called Decisive Results. They
hardly ever fail in their mission. I'm
not sure about the skill level of your
group, James, but be confident
in the skill of the one that I have
dispatched. They are all either
former Israeli Defense Force or
Moussad trained. You are as safe
as a man with a price on his head
can be.

James let out a little chuckle at that answer, which would have been more pronounced had it not been for the weight of the situation. He translated it the best he could for Kongolo, who also chuckled at that last line.

Another two hours away from Domiongo, the men stopped to rest and switch positions. Just then Kongolo got a text from Katey.

The chief and village police
located the man with the cleft
in his chin. He was arrested and
was being "questioned" by skilled
interrogators. We will pass along
any necessary information.

James handed his phone to Kongolo, who was now the passenger, and asked him to text the intel to Aharon, complete with the quotation marks. Aharon's response was immediate: they would have someone in the village of Domiongo to pick up the suspect within the next few hours. James was relieved that the man was in custody, but he wished he could have been there to question him. He knew exactly why the quotation marks had been there. The interrogators did not have a reputation for being gentle or following the Geneva Convention rules.

At this point, they were four hours away from Domiongo, and James wondered if anyone had noticed their absence or if they were already being pursued. He doubted it, but it seemed that this enemy was omnipresent. He wondered exactly how much information they had gotten during those days before he noticed the surveillance device in his room.

One more hour passed and James and Kongolo switched positions again. Both were tired, taking repeated catnaps on the back of the bike. The night, the dark jungle, and the wide-open savannah seemed endless as their fatigue grew in intensity. They wondered if they would ever reach Lodi or the Sankuru River.

Chapter 61

It was nearly four a.m. and Kongolo was driving. James was catching a quick snooze when suddenly something caught Kongolo's gaze. Just off the path to the right, something small with a deep crimson blinking light seemed to be following them.

"James! Monsieur, are you awake?"

"What is it, Kongolo?"

"There, just off to the right of the path, only a few inches from the trees. That looks like the drone that followed us when we were fleeing the rebel camp. Do you recognize it? Is it friend or foe?" Kongolo's voice was tight.

James studied the light for several minutes. One thing he did notice was that the blinking was slowing down. That could mean two things: one, the battery was dying; or two, the pace was a form of communication. He expressed this to Kongolo and asked if he thought the intervals were further apart than when he first noticed.

"Maybe," Kongolo said with little commitment. "Could that be the battery?"

"Could be. If it is an enemy drone, and the battery is losing charge, that's a good thing. If it's a friendly drone, and it's losing power, that's bad. But if it is friendly and the blinking pattern is a code, then we need to figure out what it means."

"Good points. Use your phone timer app to test the seconds between blinks. See if it is only getting slower or if the pace is changing."

James timed the pace of the drone's light. It did seem to be changing tempo. He decided it was not only a form of communication, but quickly recognized it as Morse code.

"Well, I'm not sure if it's from Caleb's team, or the one sent by Aharon, but I don't think that really matters," James said. The decision that it was friendly was a relief to both.

James watched the intervals and the order that they were being sent, translating them to the corresponding letters. It took several minutes, but finally he deciphered a sentence: Where are you? The question briefly gave him pause but he determined that the drone's camera must be infrared, and that it had likely been following the heat given off by the two bodies and the motorcycle. Since they were asking for a location, it also clearly didn't have a GPS tracker installed. He didn't have time overthink the situation and so, while it was a lot of letters to transmit, he used the light from his small flashlight and answered as quickly as he could:

```
Thirty minutes south of Lodi, on the
road to the Sankuru River.
```

Within ten minutes, the whole jungle was lit up like New Year's Day at 12:01 a.m.

Immediately, James wished that it was him up front driving. He heard loud shouting in accents that were decidedly neither Israeli nor American English, and his blood ran cold. He had made a costly mistake, communicating to an enemy drone his exact location. Just above, a helicopter was spot lighting his progress on the path. Doors opened, and men began to repel from the chopper, taking aim as they did.

"Kongolo, naponi mabe! I was wrong! This is the enemy. Open the accelerator wide and get us out of here! We need to head deeper into the jungle for better cover."

Kongolo responded instantaneously, and the Indian shot forward, leaving the group from South Africa dropping to the ground as they were rounding a bend in the road. Shots rang out, but none were anywhere close to their mark. They continued to hear gunfire, but the shots were quickly fading into the forest behind them.

"Do you know this group, Monsieur?" Kongolo asked, panting nervously.

"I think so, and it's not good."

"Who are they? Where are they from?"

"I'm pretty sure those were Afrique du Sud accents, Kongolo. I am so stupid to have assumed that the drone was friendly. I actually gave them our position. So stupid. This is a well-known mercenary group called Decisive Results. They have made it known that they'll take any job to kill anyone, anywhere, anytime, for the right price, and certainly can afford the sophisticated drone and that helicopter. Let's just hope they don't have ground transportation. If they lower a dirt bike or something newer and better equipped than what we're on, we're as good as dead."

"If the group has no restrictions with money," Kongolo yelled nervously, "I'd say it is very likely that we are in trouble. We should count on it if we want to properly defend ourselves."

"True," James agreed. "How long 'til we reach the river?"

"Why?"

James explained, "I don't want to lead a battle right into a sleeping village. I wonder if we should ditch the bike and go on foot the rest of the way. What do you think?"

"We are about twenty minutes from the south side of Lodi," Kongolo answered. After a brief pause to think, puffing a bit, he went on, "I say we ride another ten minutes at least. We can leave the bike somewhere where I can easily find it if I want to get back home this way. But if the enemy catches up to us, we will need to leave the bike earlier and hunker down for a fight, hoping our friends arrive on time. Getting you flowing south on the Sankuru is the only real goal right now." James encouraged Kongolo to continue to breathe in deeply, preparing their minds so their bodies could eventually jump into action.

They rode on for about another twelve minutes without incident and found a place to hide the Indian in the foliage. As soon as had they stepped back out onto the path to continue their trek northward, James received a text from Aharon. Seconds later, one came in from Caleb. Both groups were approaching the village of Lodi and concerned to learn that the mercenaries had beaten them to James.

Around the next bend in the road, the campfires from the perimeter houses and huts could be seen. Kongolo and James knew that they were getting close, but feared they may not reach the riverbank before their pursuers caught up with them. Seemingly out of nowhere, they both heard one, lone motorcycle heading toward them from the south and bolted for the woods near the edge of the village. They needed to find a place to take their stand.

Chapter 62

Kongolo and James took cover in the dense foliage just off the main path and looked for a place to both conceal them and give them a good line of sight to see the enemy. Kongolo found it. A rise in the forest floor came up about ten feet and was surrounded by a small area of bamboo which was close enough together to provide protection, but wide enough for the two men to fit into the little clearing.

Kongolo placed himself in front of James and began to ready his gun for the fight. Both men also had knives and the skills to use them. Once their weapons were poised, they laid perfectly still, not wanting so much as a snapped twig to give away their location.

The motorcycle, carrying only two men, stopped on the path about twenty feet from where they were. Assuming that James would not take the fight into the village, they left their bike parked just off the path and began searching the woods on the east side of the road, fortunately away from James and Kongolo, who barely breathed as they watched the men using flashlights to look for their prey.

Even though the distance was three hundred meters, and although it was still mostly dark, the flashlights in the hands of the enemy made it easy for the two in hiding to watch their movements. Neither spoke nor made a sound, but both were wondering the same thing: if an offensive attack may be their best move. James calculated how long Kongolo could hold off two South African Vektor pistols with his one weapon, and he guessed that neither man wanted to see the combat reduced to a knife fight.

They kept still as the enemy soldiers-for-hire crossed over to their side of the road. James prayed. Kongolo prayed. Both remembered the conversation about waiting and God renewing strength. They each concluded that the strategy was still their best bet. By now the two mercenaries were within fifty meters of them. Just as James was wondering if waiting would really pay off when the sound of two helicopters came into earshot. A nearly silent sigh of relief escaped both men as their searchers drew close.

The noise from the airships caused the two South Africans to look up and study to see if the helicopter was theirs. Not being able to tell, and not wanting the distraction to allow their target to slip away, they turned their backs on the helicopter and continued their search, putting them were within twenty meters. Kongolo silently motioned for James to head to the village, and he would cover him. James thought that this was a smart decision. He slowly rose to a crouching position and headed down the north side of the small embankment, hoping it was large enough to mask his movement.

James was only a short distance down the tiny footpath when a gun fight broke out all around him. Picking up the pace as a round of bullets from the semi-automatic pistols thwacked the tree ten meters behind him, he couldn't be sure if he was the intended target, so he continued his northward trajectory. The village fires were close now. Kongolo's distinct weapon was heard adding to the noise of the enemy and, for a moment, confusion completely reigned.

Just then, Caleb's group was overhead and shooting, as they descended on the ropes dropping from the helicopter. Caleb landed closest to James, while the others, led by the Congolese national, ran to back up Kongolo.

"This way," James whispered to his friend, who joined him on the path forward as the chaos ensued behind them. James shifted the saddlebags that he was carrying to his other arm. Caleb took up the rear, his full body armor blocking any possible projectiles aimed their way. They reached the edge of the village and found its citizens waking up to the sound of a battle raging just south of where they had been sleeping only moments earlier.

A villager stepped out to run behind them. "What is happening?" he asked.

James quickly explained, in Lingala, who he was and why he was running away from the people chasing him, and that he needed a canoe to take him south. The man motioned them to follow him to the huts along the edge of the riverbank. Caleb turned his back on James and readied himself to defend the village while the escape plan unfolded.

Just then, a second helicopter stopped overhead and began dropping additional soldiers. As soon as they spoke, Caleb knew that they were safe. The strong, Israeli accent identified them immediately, and he sighed with relief.

Deeper into the village, the natives helped James locate a canoe owner who could take him down river. No one had an outboard, but further downstream, at a larger village, several outboard canoes could be hired. One man immediately called his cousin to have his motor ready. Caleb barely caught a glimpse of James stepping into the boat and felt additional relief to see that one of the Israeli soldiers had caught up to him and could offer protection, should the fight come to them.

Chapter 63

Caleb turned back around to see the rest of the South African team emerging from the jungle just east of where James' canoe was being pushed off the bank. The Congolese scattered in every direction as the Israeli in the boat with James pushed him onto the floor and started shooting at the enemy within easy target range. The man took a bullet in the neck and dropped hard to the ground.

Caleb took cover behind an old canoe and was thankful for the hardwood that was often used to build these boats. James felt helpless lying on the floor, but the look the Israeli gave him demanded that he stay still. Caleb lifted himself up just enough to take a shot at the second South African. The man took the bullet in his Kevlar, but the force of the shot still brought him to his knees. The Israeli next to Caleb finished him off with a second neck shot.

By now, the Congolese steering the boat knew that the current would soon draw them away from the scene of this unprecedented, pre-dawn fight. Dark enough to have some cover but light enough to easily see the battle, James remained on the floor of the vessel until the Israeli thought they were safe around the first bend in the swiftly moving river. Even as the village faded into the background, the sound of gun shots continued, but only for a few minutes more. After one final shot, everything fell silent. The quiet was deafening. Nothing was moving.

"I think it is safe for you to sit up now, James," the Israeli soldier said as he offered a hand. "My name is Benjamin. I was sent by the committee to see that you safely reach Ilebo."

"I appreciate that," James acknowledged. "Both you and my American group have perfect timing. I don't think that I would have survived without your help. It was partly my fault." James explained about communicating with the drone thinking that it was friendly. Benjamin heard James' confession without emotion, just a nod of the head.

The man driving the boat then spoke for the first time, introducing himself as Gabby, and explained that the village where they hoped to find a waiting outboard was two hours south with the rate of the current. He suggested that James and Benjamin rest and eat. A suggestion that they both thought was a good one. Two hours, James thought. Enough time to get some information out of the Israeli, but he doesn't seem to be much of a talker.

After eating some peanuts and the sandwiches that he had

packed, and drinking some water, James attempted to text Julia, but his phone had no signal. He found a position in the boat that was as comfortable as possible considering the situation and the unforgiving craft. He was silently concerned about Kongolo and Caleb but tried to shut that off so he could rest up for what he inevitably knew was coming. Ultimately, exhaustion took over, and James managed to sleep hard for almost an hour before waking up when Benjamin touched his arm.

"The village is just a few minutes south," Gabby informed. "It is called Mapangu. My cousin is waiting with the canoe ready and fueled. I will finish my journey there." The man looked hopefully at James.

"How much do you typically charge for this trip?" James asked.

"Twenty American dollars, Monsieur. But an additional gift would be appreciated. I have four children entering ecole de classe when the vacation is finished. It is very expensive to pay for their tuition, clothes, and supplies."

James handed the man fifty dollars without question. He also inquired as to how much his cousin would charge for the rest of the trip. Gabby said that he thought he would do it for about one hundred, but did not hesitate to add that his cousin, too, had a large family and would also be appreciative of an additional gift.

Within a few minutes, James and Benjamin were meeting the

cousin, a man named Jean Luc. At the village, James was relieved to see that the bars on his phone showed he now had a good enough signal to communicate. James called Caleb first and then Kongolo. Both were safe. Caleb had given himself the task of riding back to Domiongo with Kongolo. He wanted to be sure that things were finished properly with Lucas and the medical response and informed James that a group of scientists had been found to be using the small house in Domiongo to purposefully infect lesula monkeys with the Ebola virus for testing purposes, confirming James' suspicions. He also said that the rest of the Israeli group had finished off the South African team, and that they had planned to go back to the village by helicopter to secure the man with the cleft chin. They wanted their chance to interrogate him as well. James almost felt sorry for the man. Having been questioned by the Congolese himself, he knew what that entailed and how painful it could be. Compounding that with an Israeli integragation would only add insult to injury.

He was so thankful that everything was finished, that the village of Lodi was safe, and that Caleb would ensure that the compound would be secured. Before losing coverage, James called Julia. He explained as simply as he could that he was safe, he was away from the compound at Domiongo, and that he would call her again with a longer version of the story in a day or two. As the wife of a soldier, she was practiced in the art of waiting for the details.

The day dragged on. Early morning gave way to the intense sun and heat of mid-morning. James, Benjamin, and Jean Luc covered themselves to prevent being burned. At noon, the threesome pulled onto a sand bar to rest and use the bathroom. They ate, stretched their legs, and then resumed their journey. Jean Luc predicted that it would be after dark when they finally reached Ilebo.

Chapter 64

After what seemed like forever, the outboard reached the place where the Sankuru joined the Kasai, an obviously larger river. It was already dusk. Jean Luc said that they would reach the port around seven-thirty. It would be very dark by then.

Benjamin looked at his watch. He spoke to Jean Luc in French, which put James at a disadvantage. He knew a little of that language, but not enough to keep up with the volume and pace at which it was being spoken. He finally asked Benjamin to explain what was being said.

"I was giving Jean Luc directions as to where to stop the canoe. We do not want to attract attention by arriving at the main port after dark. There is a small cement dock where we can tie up, just north of customs. That way your presence will not be easily seen. I am only to walk you a few hundred meters and then leave you. Even I am not given all information." He shrugged.

"I see," James sighed, slightly worried but too worn out to seriously care. "Do you at least know who I am to connect with?"

"I have not been made aware of the details. I simply know that my assignment was to be sure that you reach the city and find the entrance."

"Fine." As one soldier to another, James could not begrudge the man only knowing so much. That was often the case to protect the sensitivity of the mission.

When they were about twenty minutes from the destination, James paid Jean Luc and gave him extra for a hotel stay, meals, and a port fee for docking his canoe. He wanted to be ready to move when the time came.

As the cement dock came into view, Jean Luc handed the rope to Benjamin and reached out for the archaic, rusty ladder that hung off the side. Jean Luc secured the line to the dock and Benjamin hooked it through the handle at the front of the canoe. James grabbed his backpack and saddle bags and gripped the ladder with every ounce of strength he had left. With his journey nearly over, and knowing that he was almost safe, he began to crave that sigh of relief that rewarded those who persevered.

Benjamin climbed up beside him, and the two watched Jean Luc sit into the boat. He would wait until Benjamin gave the signal, and he would move the canoe to the main port to tie up for the night.

"This way," Benjamin led. "I am to take you to the entrance of a shortcut to your destination. We are very close now." He stepped out of the way and struggled to open what appeared to be a vine-covered, ancient door leading into the side of the hill. With the lights from the city threatening to give them away, this gave them the best chance to avoid detection.

"You must take this tunnel. You will follow it until you reach a wooden door, painted red, with a metal knocker. Rap it three times slowly. The tunnel travels mostly up hill. Do you have a torch, a flashlight?"

James nodded and took it out. Without saying goodbye, Benjamin turned and shut the old door behind him. James started up the tunnel, which took a sharp, vertical turn. Within five minutes, he had climbed what felt like several hundred meters. He was about to stop for a rest when he rounded a corner in the tunnel and came face to face with the door, just like Benjamin had described.

His hand was sweating profusely as he lifted the large, metal object.

Knock. Knock. Knock.

Slowly, the red door opened. He stepped into what appeared at first to be an old-world wine cellar. The niter on the walls and the old kegs showed its original use. No one appeared to be in the room at first, but then someone stepped into view and opened a second door for James. Despite the myriad of questions running through his mind, he knew he didn't have the luxury of stopping for answers.

He stepped through the second door where two men were waiting for him. The younger one, a man in his forties, came forward to greet him with a handshake. The tall man introduced himself as Aharon and explained that his wife had been contacted with the news that he was okay. He also informed James that the compound and medical response were now in the hands of good people, and that the virus should be under control within a few weeks. But what was explained next would change his life forever, not exactly what he was hoping to hear at the age of thirty-seven, one year away from his retirement. Not what he wanted to hear at all.

"We've been waiting for you, James. You are the last missing piece to our now perfect puzzle. Welcome..."

About the Author

In 2003, Chrisann Dawson found herself with a broken leg and a toddler to care for. Each afternoon during nap time, she would work on her first book, "Congo Crisis." She has since written two additional books in the series: this one and the upcoming "Congo Ebola," with plans for more.

Chrisann and her husband Gale, along with their three children, lived in the Congo, Africa (formerly Zaire) for seven years doing mission work. They learned the Lingala language, became emersed in the culture, and established lifelong friendships with the Congolese people, who continue to do the work of their non-profit mission, Rise Congo.

Chrisann now lives in Payson, Arizona, where she works part-time for the University of Arizona Cooperative Extension, doing vision and hearing screenings for preschool children in her county. She also works as a member of a chaplain team with Gale at Payson Christian Clinic, and she continues to pursue her writing dreams.

Also by Chrisann Dawson

Congo Crisis

Congo Terror

Principles and Proverbs

from

Pride and Prejudice

Relationship Secrets

of

Pride and Prejudice

www.ingramcontent.com/pod-product-compliance
Lightning Source LLC
Chambersburg PA
CBHW072010190726
48293CB00001B/221